MIND
GAMES

Also by Kiersten White

~

PARANORMALCY

SUPERNATURALLY

ENDLESSLY

MIND
GAMES

KIERSTEN WHITE

HARPER TEEN
An Imprint of HarperCollinsPublishers

HarperTeen is an imprint of HarperCollins Publishers.

Mind Games
Copyright © 2013 by Kiersten Brazier
www.epicreads.com

Library of Congress Cataloging-in-Publication Data
White, Kiersten.
    Mind games / Kiersten White. — 1st ed.
        p.   cm.
    Summary: "Seventeen-year-old Fia and her sister, Annie, are trapped
in a school that uses young female psychics and mind readers as tools for
corporate espionage—and if Fia doesn't play by the rules of their deadly game,
Annie will be killed"—Provided by pub.
    ISBN 978-0-06-213531-5 (trade bdg.)
    [1. Psychic ability—Fiction.   2. Sisters—Fiction.]   I. Title.
PZ7.W583764Mi   2013   2012004292
[Fic]—dc23   CIP
                                                                AC

Typography by Torborg Davern
13 14 15 16 17   CG/RRDH   10 9 8 7 6 5 4 3 2 1

First Edition

To Erin, Lindsey, Lauren, and Matthew—
siblings, friends, partners in crime

MIND
GAMES

FIA
Seven Years Ago
~

MY DRESS IS BLACK AND ITCHY AND I HATE IT. I WANT to peel it off and I want to kick Aunt Ellen for making me wear it. And it's short, my legs in white tights stretching out too long under the hem. I haven't worn this dress in two years, not since I was nine, and I hated it then, too.

Annie's dress is just as stupid as mine, but at least she can't see how dumb we look. I can. I don't want to be embarrassed today. Today is for being sad. But I am sad and embarrassed and uncomfortable, too.

It should be raining. It's supposed to rain at funerals. I want it to rain, but the sun bakes down and it hurts my eyes and everything is sharp and bright like the world doesn't know the earth is swallowing up my parents.

My parents. My parents. Mom and Dad.

Annie cries softly next to me, her head bent so low we're nearly the same height. I'm glad she can't see any of this, can't see the caskets, can't see the mats of fake green grass around them. Just show us the dirt. They are going in the dirt. I would rather see the dirt.

I reach out and take Annie's hand in mine. I squeeze it and squeeze it because she is my responsibility now, and no one else's. *I'll take care of her*, I promise my parents. I'll take care of her.

FIA
Monday Morning
~

THE MOMENT HE BENDS OVER TO HELP THE SORROW-
eyed spaniel puppy, I know I won't be able to kill him.

This, of course, ruins my entire day.

I tap my fingers (tap tap tap them) nervously against my
jeans. He's still helping the puppy, untangling the leash from a
tree outside the bar. And he's not only setting it free, he's talking to it. I can't hear the words but I can see in the puppy's tail
that, however he's talking, he's talking just right, all tender
sweet cheerful comfort as his long fingers deftly untwist and
unwind and undo my entire day, my entire life. Because if he
doesn't die today, Annie will, and that is one death I cannot
have on my conscience.

Why did he have to help the puppy? If he had walked by

like he was supposed to, I could have crossed the street, followed him into the alley, and ended his life as anonymously as possible.

Now he is more than a photo and a location. He is panting-puppy salvation. He is legs that stick out at grasshopper angles as he gives the spaniel one last ear rub. He is shoes scuffed up and jeans worn thin and dark hair accidentally mussed. He is eyes squinting because of forgotten sunglasses and heavy backpack throwing off his balance. He is too-big ears and too-big smile and too-big eyes and (too-big too-big too-big) too real for me to end.

I stay in the shadowed recesses across the street. Why did they send me on this one? Why couldn't it have been stealing bank account information from a CEO or blackmailing a judge? I could have done those. I do those. All the time.

I haven't messed up this bad in two years. I've done everything James asked me to, everything Keane wanted me to. I've kept Annie safe, and so what if how we're living is no way to live, at least it's *alive*. James let me come alone on this trip, and I know it's a test to see if I'm really theirs, if they can trust that my need to protect Annie cements me to them forever, no matter what horrors I'm doing. I can't mess up.

Technically I haven't yet, I could still do it, I could still keep Annie safe and sound in her room where she sees nothing but fractured visions of life. Maybe she's already seen this, maybe she knows it ended for us the moment this boy helped that puppy and became a person to me.

That dumb dog has killed us all.

But the decision is made and I have to cross the street and finish what I've begun. Now. I can't plan it. Planning isn't safe—it begs for Seers to spy on you. I have to just go.

My feet step onto the asphalt, carry me across, and I don't know what to do. For so long my brain has been trained to ignore the *wrong* pulsing constantly, trained to work in spite of knowing everything I'm doing is always bad. Now I am thinking only for myself, using my instincts for my own good.

Which, for whatever reason, means this guy needs to come with me now, somewhere I don't know yet, but I feel like north is the right direction. I am about to become the grateful owner of the silky-eared engineer of my destruction.

"You found my puppy!" A voice that is not my own but what he needs to hear slips out of my mouth, and the instant his eyes meet mine (gray, he has gray eyes, I would have closed his gray eyes forever), I know I have him for as far north as I need to go, and after that I will figure it out.

Planning is not my friend. Impulse is.

"This is your dog?" he asks, and his voice is deeper than I thought it would be and as kind and warm and untainted by violence as I knew it would be. He takes me in, my wide blue eyes, china doll lips, long brown hair: I am the picture of teenage innocence.

I lean down and pull the dog toward me. No tag on the

collar, I get to name it. "Yes! Thank you. My dad—" I hesitate and look toward the bar. His gaze follows mine and then snaps back, sympathetic color flooding his face on my behalf.

Guys are so easy.

I stand, keeping my eyes on the dog as though I can't bear to meet the boy's instead. "Well, uh, he was supposed to be back two hours ago. I got worried. Chloe needs to eat."

"I didn't find her," he says, his voice soft and bright to try and compensate for my embarrassment. "Just untangled her. She's a great dog."

My cue to look up and recover. "She is, isn't she? She's my best friend in the whole world. Oh, gosh, that makes me sound like a loser." I giggle just like I should. He smiles. (His gray eyes, they will haunt me forever with what I would have done—what I still could do—what I still should do—oh, Annie, have you already seen this? Did you know when I left that I'd kill us both?)

"No, not at all. I love dogs. I had a German shepherd growing up; I still miss him."

I twist the leash around my hand, drawing his attention there. Small hands, safe hands, hands he probably thinks he might like to hold once he figures out whether or not I'm too young for him. It makes me sick to look at my hands. "There's a deli a few blocks away where I can get something for Chloe. Do you—I mean, if you aren't doing anything, I'd love to say thank you for helping my puppy, and if you wanted to come along, I could—it'd be my treat?"

I know he's going to say yes before it comes tumbling out of his lips and I smile in shy delight. He wants to get away from the bar of my pretended shame, and he wants to get to know me better and figure out whether or not I'm old enough for him to be interested in.

What on earth can this stuttering-arms-and-legs-and-nervous-hands guy have done to get on Keane's hit list? I'll have to find out. Because I'm going against Keane (oh no, oh no, they will kill us both) and I need to know as much as I can to try and fix it. When they give me things to do, they never tell me why. Just what. They want me operating on as little information as possible. I'm not like the other girls, the ones who choose to help them, who like money and power.

They know I have no choice, but if I did, they'd all be dead.

"It's this way." I walk in the direction we need to go. It feels right, in the same way you feel a drop coming up on a roller coaster before you go over the edge. I'm falling, but I'm falling exactly how I'm supposed to.

"I'm Adam, by the way."

"Oh," I say, with another giggle. "Yeah. I'm Sofia." I almost miss a step. I told him my name—my real name. Why did it come out like that? I always lie. "My friends call me Fia, though. Or, well, I guess my dog does, since I already told you she's my only friend."

He laughs again. He likes me so much and he wants to know how old I am—I can read it in every line of his body. "Do you live around here?" he asks.

"Just visiting. Kind of a field trip, I guess." I see his eyebrows rise involuntarily and even though I am a dead girl walking I smile, really smile. He's scared now, but not of what he should be. "I'm seventeen."

A relieved exhalation. "Oh, good. No offense, but you look young."

"They always tell me I'll like it when I'm older."

"They said the same thing when I was the awkward, horrible, six-foot two-inch wonder at thirteen." He smiles, remembering, and I wonder what he was like then. I wonder what he is like now. "I'm nineteen, by the way, just in case maybe I look a lot older or younger than I really am."

"No, you look exactly like what you really are." He does not lie, this nineteen-year-old boy. With his body or his face or his mouth. My finger taps out the why-why-why of his death. "Do *you* live around here?"

"Studying, actually. At the university hospital."

"Are you going to be a doctor?" My voice is tinged with a bit of awe. I think it's right for what he thinks of me, but my eyes are tracing the lines of the empty sidewalks stretching out in front of us. I still don't know where we are going; I let the dog trot to the end of the leash.

I wonder if Keane has a Seer (other than Annie) talented enough to see me yet. I wonder how I am going to hide this from the Readers and the Feelers. I wonder how bad it will hurt to die, and if I will mind so terribly much after all.

"In a way. I'm really more on the research side than treating people. When do you graduate?"

I turn with my smile, ready to make something up, and I see them.

Three men. Dark clothes, thin jackets, nothing notable about any of them. They are not looking at us as they approach from the next street over. They are coming for him or for me or for both of us.

Dear, dear intuition: Why did you lead me in this direction? Because being ambushed by three men is not my idea of a good plan. At least they aren't women; my thoughts and emotions are still safe. Men can't get in my head.

"Come on," I say, tugging the leash and hurrying down the sidewalk.

"What kind of field trip are you on? Will you be in town for a while?"

"I have no idea. My plans changed about five minutes ago." I look over my shoulder to see the men, three (tap tap tap—I hate the number three), thick shoulders, one gun between them based on the way the guy in the middle is walking (that was a mistake, they should all have guns—guess they'll find out), matching our pace and getting closer.

Maybe I don't remember what it's like to not feel wrong all the time. Maybe without the constant low hum of pain in my head, the twist of my stomach, that feeling you get just before something bad happens that you can't know is going to happen but you know anyway, the feeling that has been my constant companion these last five years—maybe without it I'm nothing. Maybe I can only choose right when I'm choosing on someone else's orders. Maybe I am about to die even sooner than I thought.

I lean over and scoop up Chloe, burying my face in her silky fur. Okay. I can die today. If I die, they'll never know I didn't do what they told me to, and Annie will be safe. Keane can't use her to punish me if I'm dead. But I'm going to get Adam out, because otherwise this whole thing was pointless.

"In here." I veer into a narrow alleyway between looming brick buildings. It's open on both ends, good, no recessed doorways, not as good, but it'll do.

"Is this a shortcut?" he asks, looking back over his shoulder to see what I keep looking at.

I set Chloe down and unhook her leash. "Shoo," I say. She looks up at me with her sorrow eyes, and I let out a low growl from the back of my throat. "SHOO!" Tail between her legs, she scampers out of the alley and to safety.

That's one of us.

"What did you—why did you let your dog go?"

"Not my dog." I put my hands on my hips and look up into Adam's confused face. "Listen carefully. I was here today to kill you."

An unsure smile twists his lips as he shifts his weight, trying to figure out how to tell me my joke isn't funny. "Uh, that's—"

"If I were going to kill you, you'd already be dead. I don't know why you're supposed to die, I'm hoping you can tell me, but right now we don't have time because three men are about to come in the alley and either they want to kill you or me or both of us. Which sucks. So stay out of my way and I'll try to get us out."

He opens his mouth to ask what I'm talking about when the three men turn into the alley and slow down, approaching us with wary eyes and tight smiles. Their smiles are lies.

Most smiles are.

"There you are," I say. I stand in front of Adam, casually putting myself between him and the three men. Dark hair on the right—movements tight, too much muscle mass, won't be quick. Sandy blond in the middle, packing the gun, will try not to engage in hand-to-hand because he's psychologically dependent on his weapon. Stubble on the left—lean, fluid movements, my biggest problem.

They stop right in front of me, and I still haven't figured out which one of us they are here for.

"James didn't tell me I'd have backup," I say. Their eyes flicker to each other, only a split second, but it's enough. They aren't with Keane. "He really needs to warn me about these things. Would've saved me the trouble of pretending to flirt with Lurpy." I jerk a thumb toward Adam, deliberately not saying his name. "You guys got it from here?"

Sandy blond with the gun smiles, his teeth wide and white and even. "Yeah, of course. We'll take Adam with us." Bingo. They know who he is.

"What?" Adam says, his voice breaking a little on the word, like it's sharp in his throat.

Keane didn't send them, and I'm not their target, but now they probably know I'm with Keane. Well, thank you again, *north*. I really must be broken if trapping us in an alley with people who want Adam was the best I could do. "He's all yours. As soon as you tell me the password."

"The password?" Dark hair too-thick muscles answers, and I wish it were only him because he is slow.

I laugh. "Kidding. I keep asking them to set us up with code words, you know? Cooler. Oh well."

Stubble doesn't smile. He hasn't stopped studying me this whole time, and even though I know they're here for Adam (why, you stupid sweet boy, what is it about you?), I know Stubble wants me just as much now, if only to figure me out the way I'm desperate to figure out Adam.

Stubble gestures. "We've got a ride for you. One block back, on the corner of Fourth, black sedan."

"Great." I stretch my arms up like I'm exhausted and ready for a nap.

"What's going on here?" Adam asks, his voice tight with nerves behind me. He's still hoping this is some sort of elaborate joke. "I'm not going with anyone."

"Nice meeting you guys," I say, pulling my purse over my head. I throw it at Sandy blond with the gun, then drop to the ground and pull the knife out of my boot.

Dark hair is hamstrung before he realizes what's happening, on the ground screaming, clutching at his forever-ruined right leg. Out of the game. Sandy blond fumbles my purse, finally dropping it and going for his gun. I slash his right forearm—he won't aim as well with his left hand—but where is Stubble? I don't have a position on him.

Drop flat on the ground, now! I feel the whisper of a fist's breeze, then flip onto my back, kick up with both feet, and catch Stubble under the jaw. Stunned, not enough to keep him down; Sandy blond is swearing but about to pull out his gun. I flip back onto my feet, kick his hand (gun is on the ground, keep track of the gun), then a downward slam kick onto Sandy's bent knee. It cracks at the wrong angle. Now two of them can't chase us, only one left.

Arms circle me from behind, around my waist pinning

13

my arms, and my knife is useless (bad bad bad—I am not big enough for this, I knew Stubble would be a problem). Slam my head back into his? No, he'll expect it. I go limp and slip down a few inches, freeing my elbow, no leverage but it's something. I jam my knife into his thigh but, curse him, he doesn't drop me, just tightens his arm and I lose the knife.

Someone yells—Adam, Adam is still here, I'd forgotten about him—and I turn my head to see him grab the gun from the ground. Sandy blond was reaching for it, but now Adam has it and I don't know if this is good or bad because his hand is shaking so much he could kill any of us and I lied, I don't want to die, I really don't. I'm not ready for it.

Sandy blond tries to stand, pushing himself up against the wall, but Adam screams, "Stay down! And you!" He points the gun at us and he is trembling—oh please, soft gray eyes don't shoot me. "Drop her! Now!"

Stubble backs up a step but doesn't let me go—he is squeezing so tight can't breathe—spots in front of my eyes. Please don't shoot me, Adam. I want to get to know you, figure out why you are in this mess, get you out of it. I want to see Annie again. James will be so pissed if I die. I'll never get to dance with James.

"Calm down," Stubble says. "My name is Cole. We're not here to hurt you."

"Put her down!"

"Adam, lower the gun. She's the only one here who will hurt you."

"Then why did you attack her?" Adam's voice is shrill, tight with panic. My ribs, oh my ribs, they hurt.

"You're not thinking straight," Stubble—Cole—says. "She attacked us. We came in the alley to help you and she attacked us."

"But you had a gun!" He waves it wildly.

"And she had a knife. She probably has more weapons in her purse. I need you to help me. Put the gun down carefully, and then reach into my jacket pocket. There's a stun gun in there. It's nonlethal, and I'll use it only once to make sure this girl can't hurt any of us, and then we'll talk and no one else will get hurt. You have my word."

I hate stun guns, I hate them so much. LET GO OF MY RIBS. I push my feet against the ground and slam my head up into his chin because he isn't focused on me anymore. His arms loosen and it's all I need. I throw myself back and twist and I'm free, my hand slipping into his pocket as I stumble away from him (oh my ribs, my ribs hurt).

But Cole doesn't come for me; he rushes Adam and the gun. Cole has the gun now. I drop to the ground as the crack echoes through the alley and I roll toward him, stun gun out into his leg with a sound as bright as the charge, and then he is down but he won't be for long, so I stand and jam the stun gun into his chest and he convulses and I don't stop until his eyes roll back.

Adam—where is Adam—the gun went off! Where is Adam? He has to be okay. I look and he's there, leaning against the wall, face white with horror. My eyes sweep his body. There is no blood, no blood anywhere, oh thank heavens he didn't get shot.

"You're okay," I say, my shoulders slumping with relief. No, not relief yet, I turn and Sandy blond has a phone out, so I use the stun gun on him, too. He goes down faster than Cole. Dark hair is pale and vacant with shock, holding his leg, totally unaware of anything around him. He needs better training.

I pick my purse off the ground and drop the stun gun inside, then turn back to Adam. He's staring at me funny. Well, why wouldn't he be? I've shown him what my hands can do, and a small, worn-down part of me mourns that he won't think he wants to hold them anymore. I feel like I've lost something, but that's stupid. I lost it all a long time ago.

"I thought he shot you," I say.

"Fia," he says, his voice strangled. He's not meeting my eyes, looking down instead. "He shot *you*."

I look down, too, and he's wrong, there are no holes in my body, but then I look to the left and my blue sleeve is soaked dark with blood and then burning (horrible ripping tearing burning) comes, focused where the bullet went through my upper arm but radiating out through my whole left side.

Well, crap.

ANNIE
Monday Morning

~

EDEN PUTS HER HAND ON MY BACK TO LET ME KNOW where she is as she moves around me in the tiny kitchen. "Thanks for letting me crash last night. The paint smell should be better by now. Speaking of, we should do your place next. The walls are a shade I like to call blindingly depressing white."

"Pick something pretty for me."

"Of course. Also, how long are you going to stand there, smelling tea packets?"

"As long as it takes."

"Oh!" She snaps her fingers. "We need to go to the Art Institute. Fia's out of town, right? That means we can go today!"

I force a smile. I'd rather know where Fia is than be free to go on outings with Eden. But if it means getting out of this place . . . "I've been studying up on modernism. I think I have a lot to say."

"I just wish you could see people's faces when you finish waxing eloquent about the force of anger evident in the brushstrokes and then use your cane to walk away."

"Ah, but if I could *see* their faces, it wouldn't be funny. Stay for tea?"

"Nah, I've gotta go sit in on an interview for a new security guard. His name is Liam. That sounds potentially hot, right?"

"He's forty, pockmarked, and pudgy, and will instantly fill the room with so much lust you won't be able to breathe the whole time you're in there."

"Pessimist. Wait—did you actually see him?" She hesitates, then sees my grin and slaps me lightly on the arm. "Jerk. I'll come over when I'm done and tell you how blisteringly sexy he turns out to be. Love you. Bye." The door shuts softly behind her.

I hum, halfheartedly trying to force myself to see a vision of the guy, just on the off chance it'll work. Now that Eden's gone I don't have to worry about hiding my emotions so that she doesn't know how scared I am, but I'd rather think about something else anyway.

I hear the door and almost ask Eden if she forgot something, but no. It's not her.

"Hello, James," I say, taking the kettle off the stove as its shrill song pierces the air. I don't want him here today. I've woken up every day this week with a stress headache. Now my own personal stress headache is here to visit.

"How do you always know it's me?" The couch springs creak as he sits, and he'll mess up my pillows, as usual. He always puts them back wrong.

"You walk like an elephant."

"I do not."

"A cocky elephant. And you smell like a boy. You're filling up my whole room with boy smell, and just when I was about to enjoy my tea, too." That's not true. He smells like oranges and midnight. He could be a flavor of tea.

He laughs, and in his laugh I understand why he works so well with the rest of the women around here. I'm the only one immune to him; being literally blind to his charms comes in handy. Probably why he doesn't like me. That and he knows I'm more important to Fia than he'll ever be. Which makes him hate me and want her all the more.

"Why are you here?" I reach for my mug and set it on the table, then pull a packet out from the tea jar and bring it to my nose. Hmmm, oolong, sweet and green, with a dollop of honey. Still won't combat the James smell. It'll linger in here all day, making the muscles at the back of my neck tense up. Eden will rub it for me, but not as well as Fia used to. I'll ask James if she can visit when she gets back.

And I'll hate him because Fia can only come if he says so.

"Do you need any help?" he asks. I roll my eyes. I practiced for months when we were younger, Fia coaching me so I could get it just right. She was my mirror back then. Anyway, James isn't here to help me. I won't ask him again why he's come. I'll ignore it until he bursts.

I sit at the table with my hands wrapped around the mug as the tea steeps, calmly pretending that it doesn't bother me that he's here, that I'm not terrified they've figured out I lied to Keane.

"Did you know?" His voice is rough with barely concealed anger.

My stomach flutters with fear. He could be talking about something else. "Did I know what? You forget I'm not a Reader, James. Your thoughts, thankfully, are a complete mystery to me."

"Did you know Fia would get sent on the hit?"

I let out a breath, lean back heavily into my chair. Oh, Fia, Fia, what have they done with you this time? "I never *know* anything," I snarl. "How many times do I have to tell you? I don't know. I see. And the seeing with Fia is never, ever accurate, because she's constantly shifting things in her own favor and everything changes around her all the time."

"So you had no idea she'd get picked for this job."

They don't know that I lied. Which means I'm safe, but Fia isn't. "Why would you send her? What purpose can it possibly serve? You know how fragile she is!"

One of the chairs smashes to the ground and I flinch. I didn't hear him get up. He can move silently when he wants to, and it frightens me.

"You're the one who said this Adam needed to be taken out."

"And you sent *Fia*? How could you do that? I never said Fia needed to do it! I watch for threats to your father's best interests, like *you* told me to. Adam was a threat. A huge, massive, all-consuming threat. Don't you think that merits more than a seventeen-year-old girl?" How could they? How could they send Fia? After what it did to her last time . . ."

"My father thought it was the perfect real-world test for Fia. You had to have seen this coming. Can you see how she's going to be when she gets back? Do you have any idea whether or not she's in danger?"

I can feel him leaning in, too close to my bubble. He is heat and energy and anger. This is what I understand about him that the other girls don't. Everything about James underneath his looks is anger. Fia says you can lie with your thoughts and emotions, but only the surface ones. And I never see surface.

"Well, I know she doesn't die." I narrow my eyes, daring him to challenge me on that. Death was my first vision. My own death was the vision that nearly destroyed Fia before. It's the reason we're here, the reason Fia is Keane's puppet. The reason she isn't safe.

I *will* see a world in which she is safe if it's the last thing I do.

"You tell me the second you see something with Fia. If anything happens to her . . ."

I take a sip of my tea, pray he can't see my hand trembling, and raise an eyebrow. "If anything happens to her, I'll never have to see for you again because there will be nothing left in the world I care about."

"You're not the only one who cares about her."

"Do your lies really work with the Readers and the Feelers? Because I'm just a lowly Seer, and I know you're not even fooling yourself."

His phone rings, and the elephant feet are back, stomping to the door. "Screw you, Annabelle."

"No, but thank you for offering." I smile darkly as he slams the door behind him. And then I lean my head on the table next to my mug and cry. Why did they send her? What did she do? How can I watch out for her on paths I can't see?

ANNIE

Five Years Ago

~

FIA'S MAD. I CAN FEEL IT IN THE WAY HER FINGERS squeeze mine. She doesn't usually take my hand unless I hold it out to her first; she knows it annoys me, that I can find my way well enough. Besides which, we're sitting down. I don't know what she's freaking out about.

The school representative continues in his fluid voice. It sounds cultured and smart. It sounds like a future. "Annabelle will, of course, be on full scholarship. The Keane Foundation provides a generous living for all our students in world-class dormitories, everything on-site that they could need, and each girl gets one-on-one curriculum consulting to ensure the best possible education and secure the brightest career path imaginable. We believe that there are no disabilities, merely different abilities, and that our students have a core of strength untapped by traditional education."

Aunt Ellen coos, flipping through brochures that sound thick and expensive. In truth, she's probably just as relieved as I am that I'll be out from under her roof. Inheriting two sad, strange girls from her half sister was never in her life plan. But . . . I can't leave Fia. How could I leave Fia?

No. This is too good an opportunity to pass up. Maybe Fia's life will be easier if I'm not around. If she doesn't have to worry about all the things I don't see—and, worse, the things I do. Maybe a life without me is exactly what Fia needs.

And I could use a fresh start. I haven't had a vision in months. Maybe it's over. If I move away from people who know about me, maybe I can really be done with the seeing.

I don't know if I want to be, though. Because without the visions, I don't see anything at all. I still haven't figured out if they make the darkness better or worse, but that doesn't stop me from craving them.

The first one, the worst one, runs through my mind. Two years ago now. I was twelve, sitting on the couch. And then I was in a car somehow, my parents in the front seats, the radio on softly in the background with too much static—how was I in the car? What was going on? *How could I see?* I tried to open my mouth, to tell my parents I was there, I could see, I was see-ing for the first time in eight years! But nothing happened. And then everything happened—there was a horrible noise of metal twisting and groaning, glass flying everywhere, the whole world turning and spinning and smashing the car.

And my parents.

When I opened my eyes, I was back in the darkness, screaming. My parents were gone, out on a date. Fia tried to calm me down, figure out what I was talking about. I freaked the babysitter out so much she called my parent's cell for them to come right home. They never made it.

And the worst part of all, the part that haunts me the most, is wondering if seeing what I saw *caused* the accident.

Since then it's happened a few more times—sight suddenly flooding my midnight world. Broken snatches of the future, the present, or I don't even know. I don't want to know. My eyes are worthless.

"Annie," Fia whispers, startling me as our aunt talks with the man—John? Daniel? I've forgotten his name already. She whispers low enough that she knows only I'll hear. "There's something wrong with this. Something bad."

"What are you talking about?"

"He's not—I can't explain it. Don't do it. This is wrong."

"Excuse me, girls? Do you have a question?" I can hear his smile. It sounds like confidence. I wonder if he's handsome. I think he is. I wonder if I'm beautiful. Fia says I am, but she is the best liar in the world.

"Yes, actually." Fia answers him, her voice filled with fists. "I have a lot of questions. Aunt Ellen, can you wait outside?"

"I don't think that's necessary," she says, her voice pinched with disapproval. She's worried Fia will mess this up for her, that the school will realize I'm not just blind, I'm also crazy, and then they won't want me.

"No, it's no problem," Daniel/John answers. "I'm more than happy to answer Sofia's questions privately. Why don't you go meet with my assistant and get some of the preliminary forms filled out? That's the one downside to all this—so much paperwork!" He laughs and my aunt pads out of the room, closing the door with a soft snick.

"So." He sounds less professional and more amused. "What is it you have questions about?"

"This is a load of crap."

"Fia!" I hiss.

"Why would you say that?" he asks.

"I don't know." She sounds angry, frustrated with herself. "If I knew why, I'd tell you. Annie, please, listen to me. This is a bad idea. I feel sick. We should leave. We'll be fine. The school can bring in more braille texts, and we're doing okay, right? Together? We need to stay together. Please."

I open my mouth to answer her—because now I feel sick, too, only I feel sick because I want to go to this school more than I've ever wanted anything. I have nothing here. I will only ever be the blind sister, the poor blind orphan. At a school like this, I could be Annie. I could figure out who Annie is besides the blindness. But I can't leave Fia behind. Ever.

Before I say anything, John/Daniel speaks. "You feel sick about this? Can you describe the feeling?"

"No, I can't describe the feeling," she snaps. "All I know is that this is a bad idea and you're a liar and I should keep Annie far, far away from you and your stupid school."

He stands, and I can hear the smile slide back into his voice. "You're twelve, correct? You know, Sofia, we like girls with independent spirits. I can see that you two are a package deal. How would you feel about joining your sister? And I should tell you that the Keane Foundation has a lot of ties in the medical community; we would immediately start researching to see if there is a way to reverse Annabelle's retinopathy—the condition that caused her blindness."

I squeeze Fia's hand, my heart stopped. A school. A new chance. And maybe, just maybe, new eyes that would see only what they were supposed to. "Please, please, oh please, come with me. Please come with me. You felt sick about it because we were going to be separated, but now we won't! It's perfect."

"It's still wrong," she whispers, but I don't let go of her hand. I won't. I already know I'll win this, because she always lets me win, and we'll go together, and our lives will really start.

FIA
Monday Morning
~

I CHECK THE THREE MEN—ALL ARE DOWN. WE NEED to go now. "Come on."

I walk toward the other end of the alley, but Adam doesn't follow. "What just happened?" he asks.

"Please," I say through gritted teeth. "We need to get out of here. One of those guys was calling someone and I can't fight anyone else."

Adam still hesitates. He looks at the men and then at me, over and over again, like he is trying to put together a complicated puzzle.

"Please," I say again. "They're going to kill you. They already shot me. Please."

And then, his eyes wide with shock, he runs to catch up with me. He doesn't walk right next to me, but rather a few feet away and behind, wary. He's decided I'm his best option. I hope he's right.

"We need to call the cops."

"No, we can't. You need to be dead, Adam."

"I—what?"

"I don't know what those guys wanted with you. But the guys I work for want you dead. And if you aren't dead, they'll keep coming after you, and they'll kill the only person I love in the whole world to punish me for not doing what they told me to. So as far as anyone is concerned, you are dead."

He stops again. Please stop stopping, Adam, we don't have time for this. "So you really were going to kill me?" He's reacting calmly—too calmly, he's probably in shock. He regards me with a strange sort of analytical intelligence in his face. I am still a puzzle. A violent puzzle.

I want to grab my arm, I know I need to slow the bleeding, but it will hurt so much more if I touch it. "Yes. Well, no. I was sent here to kill you. But I wouldn't have. Couldn't have. Obviously. Which is why we are both in this mess now." I take a deep breath (it hurts, even breathing hurts, I wish I would pass out but I don't have time to) and look straight up into his eyes. "I work for very, very bad people. And I am going to do whatever I can to keep you safe from them. I need you to help me keep you alive, okay?"

He looks back to the alley and I can see in the lines of his body that he is still completely torn. Then his shoulders settle and angle toward me and I've won him, at least for now and *now* is where I do my best work.

"Okay," he says. "But you'll have to answer some questions."

"Believe me, I have more than you do. We need a car."

"I have a car—"

"You're dead, remember? This means no car, no ATM, no using anything that can be traced back to you." My head is spinning. I can't hear my instincts if my head's not clear. I'm already so scared that I don't know how to listen to just myself. "The other guys. They have a car waiting. We can use that."

There are so many problems. There will be no body because Adam isn't dead. But no! Cole in the alley! A whole new avenue is opening up to save me and Annie and Adam, too. North really was the right choice. Maybe my instincts aren't totally broken.

I pull out my phone with my good hand and lean heavily against the wall of the building we're in front of.

"Someone's going to see us." Adam looks around nervously. "You're bleeding. A lot." He stares at my arm, not blinking, like he's entranced. Then he shakes his head, closes his eyes, and opens them. I can see in his face he's made a decision, decided not to be freaked out. It's not what most people would do right now. I kind of love him for it. "Let me take care of your arm." He drops to a knee and pulls his backpack off his shoulder. "I have a kit in here."

"It has to look like something I could have done myself."

He nods and opens a compact first aid kit (why does he have that in his backpack? I should have one of those), pulls out scissors, and cuts away my sleeve above the wound. I don't look. I hate blood.

"I'm going to call someone. Be totally silent. He can't hear you." I push the 1 on my phone and it rings twice before James answers.

"Fia, beautiful, are you done? Do you need me to arrange a flight home?" His voice is light and easy, but there are questions there. He's worried about me; he didn't want me to do this job in the first place. I want to read into it, but I can't let myself.

"Ambushed," I say, gasping in pain at something Adam does. "I got shot."

"Where? How bad?" James tries to sound like he is all business, but I hear an undercurrent of genuine concern. Maybe I'm just pretending I do. I don't know.

"In the shoulder." I grit my teeth, then swear loudly. Adam's hands are steady and sure, and I wonder why he can be this calm over something a gun did when he was so terrified by the gun itself. "I'll live. Three guys, don't know who they were with. They weren't ours."

"Of course they weren't ours!"

"You never know. I left all three down but alive."

"And the mark?" He asks this more carefully. He knows what this will do to me. He knows, but he still couldn't stop his father from sending me.

The *mark* is carefully applying tape and gauze to keep me from bleeding too much. The mark has gentle hands that are stained with blood now, though not in the same way mine will always be. The mark is a person, and he has beautiful eyes and he helps puppies and he trusts girls he really, really shouldn't. The mark is breathing very deeply and evenly, deliberately. The mark is silently mouthing something to himself and I want to know what it is. I want to know what this boy who has to be scared out of his mind is mouthing to keep himself calm while he patches up my arm.

"Dead. Body in an alley with the three guys. I'm guessing they'll do cleanup duty since there's a lot of their own blood there and they don't want to get fingered."

"Can you get back?"

"I'll manage."

"Are you sure?"

"Yes."

I almost hang up when he talks again. "Fia?"

"What?"

"I'm glad you're okay. I'm sorry this happened."

I want to believe him. So much. "Sure you are." I end the

call. Adam puts the finishing touches on my bandage, then looks up into my face. "Congratulations," I say, smiling weakly. "You're officially dead."

He frowns, then unbuttons his black shirt and puts it around my shoulders so it covers up the bandage. He's wearing just his thin white tee now. "Can we talk?"

"Just as soon as we steal their car." I stand, wobble slightly, which is humiliating because I do not wobble, then walk quickly in the direction Cole said the car was. Adam follows, a half step behind. There's a car idling, a black sedan, with a driver. No one else. I wish I hadn't been shot, because this would be much easier.

I should go for stealth or something, anything, but I'm too tired. I walk straight up, reach down and open the driver's door (should have locked it, that was phenomenally stupid of them), and am surprised to see a woman, midtwenties, behind the wheel. She has brown hair and brown eyes and a kind face that is frozen in shock.

"You," she says, like she knows me.

I answer by grabbing the stun gun out of my purse and using it on her.

"Pull her out," I say. Adam doesn't move, so I say it again. "Pull her out."

He does, gently setting her on the sidewalk. She isn't unconscious, but she's curled up against the pain and I almost feel sorry for her.

"I should drive," Adam says, looking at my arm.

"You don't know where to go."

"Do you?"

"No, but my guess is always better than yours." My guess is always better than anyone's.

He gets in and I do, too. The seat is leather and still warm. I pull out, calmly, driving exactly the speed limit as I head east—no more north for me, thank you very much—out of the city. We're lucky. I flew here, but it's only a five-hour drive back to Chicago.

I look for OnStar, but I don't see anything. And I don't feel like the car will be traced. I don't think they'll call the police, either. I have a good feeling about this car.

"Fia." His voice is flat and I glance over to see him staring intently at me. I wish we were at a deli, eating and laughing and feeding Chloe. I miss Chloe. I wish she were my dog and I had an alcoholic father and I were the type of girl that Adam could date and rescue and fall in love with. I wish my left arm didn't hurt so much I wanted to die, because it also means I can't tap tap tap my leg, and without that fidget I don't know how to stop the thoughts and feelings flooding through me.

So much blood today.

"What do you do?" I ask, scanning the road. "You're just a student, right? I can't figure out why they want you dead. Do you have important parents?"

He leans back and rubs his forehead. "My dad is a dentist and my mom runs a day care." He swears softly. "They're going to think I'm dead, aren't they?"

"You can't contact them."

"This will kill them."

"You'll probably get listed as missing. They'll have hope. And you aren't really dead, which is the best part of their hope. It'll be okay." I want to reach over and take his hand. But I can't.

"How exactly do you define okay?"

I laugh, my real laugh, or at least the only real laugh I have anymore. It is short and harsh and it scrapes my throat.

He sighs. "I'm not a student. I'm a doctor."

"How old *are* you?" I shouldn't be hurt that he lied about his age, but I am. And also bothered that I hadn't been able to tell he was lying. That's bad.

"I'm nineteen." (Ha! I was right. He's not a liar.) "I just did everything faster. I moved here to finish up a research project on tracking and diagnosing brain disorders through a combination of chemical analysis and MRI mapping."

I make a noncommittal noise. I have no idea what any of that means or why it makes him need to die. I need to focus on driving.

I almost pass out on the freeway on-ramp.

We pull over and I let Adam drive. I'll figure out a place for him to hide in Chicago. I have to go home so they don't suspect something is wrong. I don't know the rest of what to do yet, but it consists of kidnapping Annie and then all of us running away together. (Stop thinking about it. No thinking.) Assuming *they* don't already know what I am planning. I could be dead as soon as I get back. I hope Annie doesn't see it, hasn't seen it, won't see it. I don't want her to see it.

But if they kill her first, I will kill as many of them as I possibly can before I go down.

"Who are you?" Adam asks after a few minutes' calm. I don't usually like riding in the passenger seat, but today it feels nice. Adam gave me something from his first aid kit that has dulled the pain enough for me to handle it. It feels nice to be dulled. Dull, dull, dull. Usually I am sharp. Being sharp all the time is exhausting. I want to take all the rest of the pills from his case.

"I'm Fia. I told you."

"I saw you back in that alley. You were crazy. You took out three guys, and you're this small girl. You look so nice and so pretty"—he blushes and I smile, oh he is adorable I wish, I wish, I am not nice—"and I don't understand what you were—what you are—any of this."

He doesn't understand. He can't. "I have to do what they tell me to. I have no choices. As far as the alley, I happen to have very good instincts." I yawn, pulling my legs up and resting my head against the seat. I am safe with Adam, for now.

"Three big guys with weapons. That's more than very good instincts."

"Okay," I say, closing my eyelids because they are heavy, heavy, heavy. "I have *perfect* instincts. And my sister can see the future. And my boss's secretary can read minds. And my ex-roommate can feel other people's emotions."

"Please don't lie to me." He sounds sad. I don't ever want to make him sad.

I feel heavy and light at the same time and I just want to sleep. I'll sleep. "Who said I was lying?" I mumble before letting go.

Everything hurts. I can't tap tap tap my fingers because something happened to my left arm and it is nothing but pain now, bright, swimming pain. I crack my eyes open and—

Oh no. Oh no, oh no. I didn't do it. I didn't kill Adam. He's sitting next to me, driving (I let him drive? Why did I let him drive?) and very much alive.

Annie, please be okay. I'll figure this out and I'll save Annie and Adam can be safe, too, because now that I remember I didn't kill him, I also remember that I'm glad I didn't kill him. It was the right choice. I'm not sure how it'll end up being the right choice, just like north getting me shot was the right choice, but I know it's the right choice.

I giggle. I can't help it. My arm hurts so bad and I got shot and I'm riding toward James in a car with the boy I was supposed to kill but didn't and my entire world is shot and I'm going to have to figure it out really fast or we'll all be dead.

"You're awake," Adam, says, looking over at me with surprise in his soft gray eyes.

"You have pretty eyes. I'm glad you're not dead."

"Uh, yeah, me too."

"I feel fuzzy."

He shifts uncomfortably, eyes on the road. "I might have overdosed you. Just a little. I needed to think."

Hmm. He drugged me. That's interesting. I felt like I was safe with him. I still do. My instincts are totally cracked from years of misuse. Maybe I'm trying to kill myself? I'm not brave enough to try again in real life, but maybe my subconscious is braver than I am and it's trying to do me in.

Oh! Adam has long eyelashes. Long arms. Long legs. Long fingers. Everything about him is long. Eden would make a dirty joke. I giggle imagining it.

Focus, focus, focus. "You drugged me."

"I almost pulled over at three different hospitals. You're bleeding through the bandaging."

I look down at the black sleeve of his shirt; it's wet. "Ruined your shirt. Sorry." I giggle again. I haven't giggled in years. Maybe I should let Adam overdose me more often. It's nice.

"I'll get a new one."

"Why didn't you pull over? Or call the cops?"

He's quiet for a while, knuckles tight on the steering wheel. "Because I've been trying to figure it out. I believe you—about the hit—I probably wouldn't if those other guys hadn't showed up, but it's all too weird to be fake. Plus I, uh, looked through your purse. Another knife in the lining, along with a few thousand dollars. Four different IDs. Is that picture of you and Annie?"

I sigh. "Yes."

"She's the one they'll hurt if you mess up."

"I already messed up. She's the one they'll hurt if I don't fix this. Wait, how do you know her name?"

"You talked. I mean, when you were out. I asked you questions, and you answered them."

I glare suspiciously at him. "You should know I lie all the time." Most people lie with words; I lie with my whole body. I lie with my thoughts and my emotions; I lie with everything that makes me who I am. I'm the best liar in the whole entire world. I hope I lied to him, whatever he asked. "What did I say?"

"Have you really killed three people?"

Tap tap tap I need to tap tap tap I need to get out of this car. I can't breathe. "Why didn't you stop at a hospital?"

"I know why I'm in the middle of this."

Why is he still talking to me? He should be scared, he should get away from me. "Oh?"

"My research. What I've been working on. I told you it was with MRI and tracking chemicals in the body to examine brain disorders, right? What I didn't tell you is there's a very specific focus. I'm mapping the brain functions of people who claim to have psychic abilities. It started as a focus inspired by this crazy aunt on my mom's side, more to disprove it than anything else, but, well, there were patterns. Specific areas of the brain more active than others, certain chemical markers present. Only in women. So I was going to expand it—start gathering information on huge segments of the population to see if I could find the same patterns in women who don't claim to be psychic."

I close my eyes, rest my head against the window. If they had that information, if they could access medical records and find women without depending on sketchy news reports or rumors or the muddled visions of their Seers, they could find all of them. No one would be safe.

"They shouldn't want to kill you," I whisper. "You're their dream come true." And now I know I have to keep him hidden no matter what, because if Keane knew, if Keane got him . . .

"I'd really like to look at your brain," Adam says.

I snort. "That has got to be the weirdest thing anyone has ever said to me."

"I mean, in an MRI. I'd like to run some tests. On you and on Annie, if I can, if she's really psychic like you say she is. What is it you can do, again? I wasn't clear on it." He runs a hand through his hair, and I see why it has that messy look. "I'm not really clear on any of this, honestly. I was still viewing it as a specific set of mental disorders that we could actually see in a scan. But if it's all *true* . . ."

"It's all true. Promise. And there's nothing special about my brain. If you scanned it, you'd probably see a swirling black mass." I close my eyes and imagine my brain. It'd be dark, all of it, black and red with bright shining spots you'd want to cling to, but all they'd do is illuminate things I never want to see again. My brain scan would give him nightmares.

"But you said you had perfect instincts."

"I'm nobody. I'm collateral damage with a lot of training." Chicago looms up ahead of us, old buildings and new buildings and cars and trees and lake, and I am so tired and my arm hurts so much and I have to go home and somehow keep my thoughts and emotions safely hidden.

No problem.

"As soon as we get into the city, pull over and get out. You can take the cash in my purse. Let me see your wallet and your phone."

He pulls them out of his pocket and I check his phone. He hasn't called or texted anyone. Good boy. I open the window and fling them both out as far as I can.

"Hey!"

"Hey nothing. Keeping you alive, remember? And if you

want to stay that way, you have to do exactly what I tell you with zero deviation. Find the cheapest hotel you can. I don't want to know where or which one. Set up an email account—chloethedog@freemail.com, password north1—and email yourself. I'll check it and we'll set up a meeting. I don't know when I'll respond, but I will. I can't plan things too far in advance or the Seers watching me will pick up on it. If they haven't already."

"Do you do this often?" he asks, his brow furrowed.

"Only for you. Don't screw it up. Don't forget you're dead. I'm risking everything here. Do you understand that?"

He pulls over; we're in an outlying neighborhood, the buildings old brick, the trees not quite blooming and budding yet. It's windy. And cold.

Turning all the way toward me, he nods. His face is open and innocent, and I know he couldn't lie if he tried. "You saved my life, Fia. Or spared it. Whichever. I'm not going to do anything that would risk yours."

I smile tightly. "I'm glad you stopped to pet the dog." Then I get out. The wind hits me and makes my arm hurt even more as we get out and pass around the front of the car. I peel off the shirt and hand it to him with an apologetic shrug. I can't show up in it. I don't look down at my arm (the blood, I hate the blood, at least it's mine this time).

"So, I'll talk to you soon, then?"

"If I'm not dead," I answer brightly, then, on impulse, which is how I live my life, I go on my tiptoes and kiss him on the cheek. It feels . . . nice. Really nice. I wish I could keep that emotion, treasure it up inside, try to figure out what it means to me. But it's not a safe emotion to bring home.

I get back in the car and drive toward the single most dangerous place in the world for me right now. I should be terrified. I should turn around and go anywhere else. I should curl up in a ball and cry. Instead, I think about everything in the whole entire world that makes me angry—there is a lot, oh, there is a lot—and I start singing Justin Bieber at the top of my lungs.

I can do this.

FIA

Four Years Ago

~

"IT'S NOT FAIR." I STAND, FEET PLANTED, ARMS crossed. I will not be scared of Ms. Robertson. I don't care how broad her shoulders are, how tight her bun is, how many students whisper that she knows you're cheating without even looking at you. She doesn't scare me (she does, and I hate it).

"What's not fair?" She raises a thin eyebrow at me.

"Why is my test all essays? Everyone else has multiple choice!"

She smiles; it doesn't touch her eyes. It is a lie of a smile. She is a liar. Everyone here is a liar. I hate this place, I hate it, it's wrong, every day it's wrong and I feel sick all the time. I hate the two postcards Aunt Ellen has sent us in the three months since we came here, saying she's in Egypt and isn't it great that the school will do all holidays and summer breaks for us. I hate the beautiful dining room with the fancy food, I hate the laundry room with the spinning washing machines, I hate the classrooms with too few students and too much attention.

Annie loves it all. She has a private tutor. They've talked with a geneticist about her eyes. She is happy.

"Well, Sofia, part of our goal at this school is to challenge our students. And you have demonstrated that you excel at multiple choice. You never miss a question. Ever. On any test in any subject."

"Are you accusing me of cheating?" I don't break eye contact. I won't. I have never cheated in my life.

"Of course not. I'm simply saying you have an uncanny knack for answering multiple-choice questions. If everything comes easily, how will you ever learn?"

I barely hold back my eye roll. Annie wouldn't approve. She tells me to roll them as much as I possibly can and makes me tell her when I'm rolling them at her. But Annie doesn't understand. She's not sick all the time, doesn't have these thoughts bouncing around in her skull making her crazy. She doesn't feel like the bottom has just dropped out of the room, like she can't quite get enough air to breathe. I do, ever since we came here. I'm crazy. But I am not a cheater.

"Fine. Whatever." I stomp back to my seat, my stupid plaid skirt swishing. The girl I share a table with, Eden, scowls. There are only five of us in the thirteen-year-olds' class. I don't get to know them. I don't want to. I wish I had classes with Annie.

"Stop being so angry all the time," she whispers. "It's distracting."

"Why do you care?" I hiss. "I'm not mad at you!"

"No, but it's . . . I don't like feeling that way. Just calm down."

Everyone here is insane. I am the insanest of the insane. I'm going to run away tonight. I'm sick of the way the staff stares at me like they're seeing straight into my head, and I'm sick of the bizarre classes they've "designed" specially for me that have me picking stocks instead of learning math, and practicing self-defense instead of gym. And I am *so sick* of feeling sick all the time.

But Annie is happy. She loves her staff mentor, Clarice, and the loads of braille texts and the pamphlets of information from the doctor I have to read out loud to her over and over again. She's bonded with Eden and they hang out constantly; you'd think *they* were sisters. She'll be happier here without me dragging her down. Maybe Eden is right—maybe I am so angry that other people can actually feel it.

I'm going to leave. I have no money. Whatever. I'll figure it out. Just planning to leave tonight I feel better already, lighter, not as jittery in my own head. There's a camera and an alarm and a security guard at the main entrance to the huge school building. But a window on the second floor has a balcony under it. Ten-foot drop. I can do a ten-foot drop. Then I'll climb the rest of the way down. The brick is old and uneven. I can do it.

I know I can.

I'm going to get out of here tonight, and I'll never come back. I'll walk back to my aunt's house if I have to. I'll live there by myself. I'll send Annie stupid postcards, and maybe they'll fix her eyes and she'll even be able to read them by herself. I don't want to be without her—that idea makes it even harder to breathe—but I can't stay here.

I look up to see Ms. Robertson smiling at me, and this time the smile isn't a lie. It's a challenge. Like she knows what I'm planning.

But she can't know.

She knows. It's a physical reaction in me, a certain quivering, empty feeling in my stomach, that tug of my gut. I *know* she knows. How does she know? I have to go now. NOW. I stand, knocking my chair over with a clatter into the table behind me. "I feel sick," I say, leaving my stuff as I run out the door. Down the long hall, all tile and dark wood. Into the residence wing. Up the stairs that smell like lemon furniture polish. Straight to the window, the one I opened last week to see how far the drop was.

It's nailed shut.

Screw this, I am gone. I sprint up another flight of stairs to the dorms with their warm yellow lights and plush red carpet. I will grab everything I own and I will run straight out the front doors. I will run into the sunshine and I will never come back here where everything is *wrong* for no reason. I burst in, and Annie's there, on the couch, and she's crying.

"What's wrong?" I ask, out of breath. "What happened?"

She looks up, but she's smiling. Why is she crying and smiling at the same time?

"I'm not the only one," she says. "Fia, it's not just me! Clarice can do it, too. Clarice sees things before they happen. And she's going to help me learn to do it better, to control it. Oh, I knew this school was the right choice." She stands and holds her hands out for a hug and I stumble forward, letting her wrap me up because I never stay away when she wants me close. "Think about it, Fia. If I had known how to control it before, I could have seen Mom and Dad earlier, I could have understood what I was seeing, I could have . . ." I know what she saw because she's told me so many times, crying in the middle of the night.

She saw their lives smashed out of them. She still blames herself because she saw the accident and didn't change it. (She didn't change it. I am here because—no, stop.)

Maybe this school *is* the best thing that ever happened to her; she can figure out how to deal with what she sees. But why do I still feel so wrong when she's so happy and hopeful? No. It's my job to take care of her. If staying here is what she needs, I'll stay.

The hairs on the back of my neck prickle and I turn to see what Annie's eyes can't. Ms. Robertson is standing, perfectly silent in the doorway, watching me.

It's been two weeks since the window was nailed shut. Bars were installed on all the windows, on all the floors. The administration said it was because of an attempted break-in.

Every day Annie chatters to me about what she learned, how smart Clarice is, what an amazing coincidence it is that she'd end up with the one person in the world who could understand her. I do not smile because with Annie I don't have to, but I lie when we are together.

Now I am sitting in class.

I am not doing any of my assignments.

I sit perfectly still and straight, and I do not work, and I do not answer questions, and they do not do anything to me. There is no detention. There are no threats. Except in self-defense, where my instructor hits me and hits me until I finally block and hit back.

I am riddled with bruises under my stiff white shirt that smells of bleach and makes me miss my mom with an ache I didn't think I could feel anymore.

I do not tell Annie. I cannot tell Annie. Annie is happy, and I have to let her be happy. It is my job to make sure Annie is happy.

I glare at Ms. Robertson, standing in the front detailing the upcoming ski trip; I still blame her for the nailed-shut window, though I have no reason to.

Then I have an idea. Maybe Clarice isn't a coincidence. This school is wrong, I know it is. I want to know why, because if I know why, then maybe it won't make me feel sick all the time. If there's a reason why it's wrong, then I am not crazy for feeling this way. (I'm not crazy, I'm *not*.) I lean back in my chair, stare straight at Ms. Robertson's forehead, and think, *I have a knife in my shoe. I have a knife in my shoe. I have a knife in my shoe, and I am going to pull it out and stab Eden. I am going to stab her until she screams. I have a knife in my shoe. I'm going to stab Eden. Right now.*

Ms. Robertson sprints down the row and rips me out of my chair, knocking me to the ground; my head slams against the floor. She pins me, it's not hard—I am all elbows and knees and I am only thirteen. She yanks off one of my shoes and then the other, breathing hard. My face is smashed into the tile. I can't see anything. I can't move.

My teacher swears. "What—why would you—Eden! How is Sofia feeling right now?"

"I don't know! How can I—"

"Just tell me how she's feeling right now!"

"She's—she was totally calm before you grabbed her. And now it's like, I don't know, like she's laughing inside, but she's also really scared." Eden sounds scared, too, having to admit that she knows this.

Ms. Robertson stands up, and I roll over onto my back, tears streaming down my cheeks from the pain in my head, but Eden's right—I'm laughing.

I laugh and laugh and laugh, and I think about stabbing Ms. Robertson with the knife I don't have in my shoe. Lighting this whole room on fire with the matches I don't have in my pocket. Hanging myself in my room with the rope I don't have in my closet.

This place is wrong, I think at her, *and I know.*

"Very clever," Ms. Robertson says, with that lie of a smile. "It would appear you're ready for the advanced placement track."

ANNIE
Monday Afternoon
~

SHE SHOULD BE BACK BY NOW. WHY ISN'T SHE BACK?
I need to hear her, to figure out if she's okay. She'll lie to me, of
course, but I still need to hear her.

It's my fault. Again. Either I see things and I can't stop them,
or I cause them because I see them wrong. I will be the death of
my entire family. I've already destroyed Fia by dragging her to
this school with me. I can't kill her, too.

I walk to the door and out into the hall. Someone stands up
immediately—Darren, by the sounds of it. He has a particular
way of exhaling whenever he has to actually do something.

"Can I help you, Miss Annabelle?"

"Why yes, Darren, you can! There's a window at the end of
the hallway, right?"

"Yeah."

"Can you open it?"

"Are you too warm? I can have the AC adjusted."

"Oh, no, the window isn't for me. It's for you. So you can throw yourself out of it."

A pause and then, "You have such a sense of humor, Miss Annabelle."

"Well, I only have the four senses, so I've got to compensate somehow. You are welcome to keep sitting in your chair, reading your romance novels. I'm going to see Eden."

"Let me know if you need anything."

"So you can disappoint me yet again by never listening? Please, Darren." I continue down the hall, tracing a hand along the smooth wood paneling, counting the seams. Skip an empty door. Skip another. Knock.

The door opens and she reaches out immediately for my hand. "What's wrong? What happened?"

"They sent Fia on a hit."

Eden swears. "Is she okay?"

"I need you to get a feel for her when she gets back. She'll lie to me."

She sighs and her grip changes as she shifts to lean farther away from me. "I'm sorry she had to do that. Really. I think it's wrong. But I can't handle being around her. You have no idea what it's like since we came back, getting sucked into all that anger. It gives me a headache. My whole mouth tastes like I'm chugging battery acid. She's poison."

"My sister is not poison." I yank my hand back.

She swears again, her voice softer. "Sorry. Just—I can already tell you how she'll feel. She'll feel angry. It's the only way she's felt since we left Europe. I wish I could help her, but I can't, and neither can you."

"Why are you even still here?" I'm so furious I want to shake her, and I know she can feel it. "Why did you come back? Why didn't you go out into the world to be Keane's little spy?"

I don't have to be a Feeler to hear the hurt in Eden's voice. "I didn't want you to be alone."

"How can you work for them?" I whisper. "They keep me here, prisoner, to control Fia."

"Did you ever think that maybe they keep you here to keep you *safe* from Fia?"

"That's a lie."

"You can't feel her like I can. She's dangerous, Annie, and it scares me every time she's alone with you. She's—" I hear her inhale sharply. "Good news, she's here. I can feel her from the first floor. Guess Art Institute is out. Come over after she's gone and we'll do manicures, okay?" Eden starts to close the door, but hesitates. "I'm sorry." Then it clicks shut.

I turn expectantly toward the elevator end of the hall. I wish I could go straight down to meet her, but unlike Eden who can come and go as she pleases, without Darren's key card I'm not allowed off the floor.

To keep me safe. Right. I am the safest prisoner in the entire world.

I strain, listening for the hum of the elevator, the muffled ding, the slide of its doors. The sound of Fia's feet stomping down the hall. She always walks loud, just for me.

But instead of sounds, I'm greeted by a flash of light and I can see—oh, light, I can see!—and it's all lights and darkness, flashing pounding lights and vibrations and everything is dark and there's smoke and it's a fire? It must be a fire! There are too many people, they'll all die—

No, it's not a fire, the bodies are dancing, the vibrations are the pounding rhythms of a song. The lights change color so quickly I can't remember their names. And Fia—oh, Fia, you are so beautiful it makes my heart hurt—is in the middle of it all, slamming her body, moving and swaying and dancing to the beat in a way that no one else can. Her eyes are closed and her arm is raised. Only one arm, she's hurt; how did she get hurt? Is this soon? But she has lost herself and I know that there, in that moment, she's happy.

I want to do nothing but stay here and watch my sister dance.

But then I know I'm not the one watching her. Someone else is. That's the point of this vision, not to see Fia happy but to see that someone else is seeing her. I try to turn to scan the crowd, but it doesn't work like that: I'm locked in, stuck seeing and only seeing but never seeing enough. Someone is watching her. Fia dances on, oblivious.

If I can just figure out who is doing the watching, then—

"Annie! Annabelle!"

Fia's voice pulls me out of the light and the darkness slams in all around me again, permanent, claustrophobic after my brief foray into vision.

"What did you see?" James's voice is terse. Crap. I should have been in my room. He wouldn't have known I saw anything. I don't tell them about the majority of what I see. That's the glory of your power being in your head and your head alone. They can't get it there.

"Fia. Dancing."

"Whoop! I'm going *dancing*!" I can feel her stomping around me in a circle, then her steps falter and something thuds into the wall.

"You are going to bed," James snaps.

"Ooh, James," Fia whispers dramatically. "Not in front of my sister. *She hates you.*"

"Are you okay?" I reach out for her, but she dances away from my grasp, humming under her breath. Some obnoxious pop song. Doris must be here—I missed everything when I was seeing.

"I'm not getting anything from her," Doris snaps. "I'm going back to my office." She walks away, muttering about having that song stuck in her head all day now.

"Baby baby *baby*, Ms. Robertson! Ta-taa!" Fia doesn't take my hand, she never does anymore, but I hear her stomping toward my room and I follow.

Her steps jerk to a halt. I assume James grabbed her. His voice is deliberately calm. "Okay, Fia. You saw her. I don't know why you needed to, but you've seen Annabelle now, so can we please get you to Dr. Grant?"

"Dr. Grant? Why does she need a doctor?" I ask.

"But I have to tell Annabelle all about my great adventure. Annie—" She leans in so close to my face I can feel her breath. "I got *SHOT*. It was awesome. How many seventeen-year-olds can say that?"

"Someone *shot* her?" I turn toward James's voice in horror. "You let her get shot?"

"Please, Fia," James says.

"Oh, fine. I also killed some poor innocent college kid. You would have liked him, Annie. He was cute. He had long legs and long arms and gray eyes. Then he was dead. Poor cute dead kid."

I let out a breath I didn't know I was holding. It felt like I'd been holding it since I lied to Keane. "I'm sorry."

"That I almost got killed or that I did some killing? 'Cause I'm not sorry about any of it. Not sorry, not sorry, not sorry at all. Is the hall spinning for anyone else? Just me? Okay, I'm gonna go get blood on Annie's couch. Don't worry, James—she can't see it. She'll never know."

I hear her shoulder dragging along the wall as she stomps—lurches—stomps to my room.

"Did you give her something?" I ask. I assume she isn't bleeding to death or James wouldn't have let her come up here at all. Maybe he gave her something for the pain already? I didn't smell any alcohol on her breath. She hasn't been this bad in a long time.

"No." James has the audacity to sound sad. He has no right to be sad about what this is doing to my sister. I take another step toward my apartment, and he brings his hand down on my arm. I shrug away from it.

"She's not allowed to be here right now."

"James. She got shot. She killed someone. I think you can afford to bend the rules."

He's quiet and I hold my breath: please, please be a person, just this once. "Fine. I'll send Grant up to take care of her in your rooms. But then she's got to go." I hate him. I hate that Fia can only visit me when they say so, that we can't ever leave this floor of the school together. That Fia can live somewhere else while I am kept locked up.

"You're a saint." I bite off the words, wishing I could be the poison to him that Fia is to Eden.

"For what it's worth, I really am sorry. About everything. And

I promise I won't leave her alone tonight. I'll take care of her."

"She's not yours to take care of." I walk to my room without tracing the wall and slam the door shut. "Fia? Where are you?"

A muffled sob comes from the couch. I trip on the corner of it and swear. I haven't tripped on my furniture in years. Then I nearly sit on her legs as I try to sit next to her. "Shh, it'll be okay."

"It won't be okay. Annie, what I did . . . what I did . . . I'm so sorry. I'll fix it, I promise."

I find her hair and stroke it; it's soft but at the end it's hard and crusted with something. Blood. I want to throw up. My baby sister is on my couch and she has blood in her hair and I don't know if it's hers or his.

"Did you see anything?" she whispers. "Are they going to kill us? Are we still okay?"

"We're fine, we're fine, I promise, we're fine." I wish I could see her arm, see how bad it is. Look in her face to see how much pain she is in. Maybe I don't wish it, actually. I'd rather see her dancing.

Which reminds me. "Don't go dancing."

She laughs. "Why?"

"Someone watches you."

She laughs again. It's harsh and low and nothing like the way she laughed when we were little. "When I dance, *everyone* watches me."

I sigh, lean my head against hers. "And don't let James stay at your place tonight."

"Did you see something? Is something bad going to happen?" She sounds terrified.

"I'm your big sister. I don't have to see anything to know James is always something bad."

Fia snorts. "You wouldn't think so if you could look at him." Then her voice is muffled as she moves the pillow back, brushing my face with it. She screams into it, then sobs, then throws it with a thud across the room. "My arm really hurts," she whimpers. I hear her finger tapping on the couch cushion, the three-then-pause-then-three in an unending loop. Oh, Fia.

"I know. But it's okay. You're done. I won't let them make you do that ever again."

"Annie," she says, hooking one hand behind my neck and pulling my head down to her lips. "I didn't do it."

"Didn't do what?"

"I'll fix it, I promise. You'll be proud of me, I'll make you proud, and I'll get you out. I didn't do it. I couldn't. I didn't kill Adam."

My heart freezes, and I grab her by the shoulders. She yelps with pain. "You didn't?"

"No, I couldn't! I'm sorry. I know I screwed up. But I thought . . . I hoped . . . you wouldn't have wanted me to kill him. He's nice, Annie. I made the right choice. I listened to myself for the first time in years. I was so scared I'd come back and you'd be—that they'd know, and they'd hurt you. But they don't know. I got away with it. And I'm going to keep listening to myself. I can do this." She waits for me to answer, but I don't, I can't. Her voice is even more pained when she talks again. "I thought you'd be proud that I saved someone Keane wanted dead."

I let her go and sink back onto the couch. A sharp knock raps on the door. "Keane didn't want him dead," I say.

The doorknob clicks; our talk is over. At least Dr. Grant is a man and therefore our minds are safe for now.

"Who then?" Fia asks, her voice slipping. She is in so much pain it hurts me to hear her, but I can't go to her, I can't help her. "Who wanted him dead?"

I stand and move away from the couch. "I did."

ANNIE

Three Years Ago

~

"I SAW THE LAKE! I CAN'T BELIEVE IT. DOES IT ALWAYS look that amazing? I can't wait to go!"

"But you won't actually be able to see it," Fia says, slamming a drawer shut.

"No, but I'll be able to remember seeing it in my vision! I can pull it all up and play it out in my mind, and I can match what I remember seeing with how it all smells and feels and sounds." I throw a pillow, jumping on her bed. I feel like I could fly. I feel like I *am* flying. I saw something because I thought about it hard enough, and it wasn't horrible or confusing. I still don't have many visions, and can't usually figure out what they are anyway—people I don't know, places I can't recognize. None as bad as the one with my parents but none particularly awesome.

But this one! It was the beach, a beautiful narrow stretch of pale sand on the shore of the lake, a lake so wide—melting off into the horizon—it might as well be the ocean. My classmates—I saw some of them, too, but the only one I recognized was Eden because of her wild curly hair that I play with when we're hanging out. And Clarice! I saw Clarice; I knew it was her because I heard her voice and I'd know her voice anywhere. Her hair is long and her eyes are blue, the same color as the sky. I had forgotten to miss blue. Blue!

I flop down onto my back, tracing my stomach happily. "I didn't tell you the best part."

"Oh?" Another drawer slams. "I can't find my bra," she mutters.

"The best part is, I saw you."

"So? I'm not that great to look at."

"Don't be stupid! This is the first time I've seen you since you were a toddler! Your hair is so shiny, and your face. Oh, Fia, you're beautiful. You're so, so beautiful. I knew who you were the second I saw you." Tears trace from the corner of each of my eyes. I'm on Fia's bed, and it smells like her, sweet vanilla, and now I know what look goes with that smell.

She was there, on the beach ahead of whatever vantage point the vision gave me, and she looked back for a brief second before kicking a ball wildly and chasing after it through a group of adults.

She didn't look happy. I wonder if she always looks that way and I don't know. Or maybe I don't remember what happy looks like. But even with her brows knit together and her mouth pulled tight, she was so beautiful. And when she ran, she was every description of graceful I have ever read.

"*You're* beautiful," she says with a sigh. "And I'm glad you saw something happy. Really. That's amazing. I hope you keep seeing happy things. It makes everything worth it."

"Maybe next time they take us on a Broadway trip I can see the show beforehand and ruin the whole thing for you."

Fia lets out a dry laugh. "You do that. I hate musicals anyway."

Our door flies open. "Where were you in class today, Fia?" Eden says, and then they both swear loudly and I feel a blanket get ripped out from underneath me.

"KNOCK FIRST!" Fia screams. I've never heard her so angry.

I wave a hand lazily in the air. "Relax! Eden doesn't have to knock. Oh, wait—are you naked? Did she see you naked?" I giggle, still giddy with happiness, still seeing the beach. I know what Eden looks like. I want to touch her hair again; it was so wild in my vision. Now when she comes over, I don't have to imagine what I think she looks like. I know! "Does Fia have big boobs? She won't tell me, and apparently it's not okay to feel them and see for myself." No one laughs. "Sheesh, joking."

"What happened to you?" Eden says. She sounds scared.

Fia stomps to the door. "Shut up. Get out of our room."

"What's wrong?" I sit up.

"Her body . . ." Eden says.

"I SAID SHUT UP."

"No, tell me what's wrong. Eden, what can't I see? What's wrong?"

"She's covered with bruises and cuts! Her whole stomach, and her arms, too! What have they been—"

"Get out of my room!"

Eden shrieks and I hear footsteps tumbling over each other, then the door slams and Fia's breathing is heavy.

"What was she talking about?"

"Nothing. Eden's an idiot. I hate her."

"She was not talking about nothing!" I stand, reaching out for Fia. She always comes when I reach out for her. But my hands meet only air. She's staying away from my hands.

She's never stayed away from my hands before.

"Are you really covered with bruises and cuts?" It comes out a whisper. I shuffle forward, and finally I connect with her. She doesn't move. I pull the blanket away and tenderly reach for her stomach. It's smooth. I trace my fingers along and she hisses a sharp breath, and there, under my fingers, on her ribs, the rough ridge of a cut. There, higher, another one. I pull her arm to me, she's been wearing long sleeves all the time—why hadn't

I noticed that? A long cut down her forearm, another on her shoulder.

"How did this happen?"

"Training," she says, and her voice has no life.

"What kind of training?"

"Lately it's been knife fighting."

"They have you learning knife fighting? I thought you were in a gymnastics and self-defense class!"

"They take it very seriously here, apparently."

I'm squeezing her arm, maybe I'm hurting her, but I can't let go, I can't let go because then I can't see her at all. She sighs.

"They're training me to fight. The knives are new. Before it was just hand-to-hand."

"Like karate?" Karate would be okay. Kids take karate all the time. Not with *knives*, though.

"Like street fighting. They have real knives. I have a plastic one. I don't get to stop until I've delivered an incapacitating blow. Doesn't matter how many times I get cut."

"*No.*"

"It's okay, Annie. I don't get cut much anymore. These are old. They're almost all healed. And I'm getting very, very good." Her voice sounds like the knives I can see sliding across her skin, through her skin, her pretty, pale skin, pale like the sand on the beach where I saw her.

"Why didn't you tell me?" I back up, pulling her with me,

until my legs hit my bed and I can sink down. My fingers trace and trace and trace the lines on her arms.

"It's not a big deal."

"It *is* a big deal! It's a huge deal. I can't believe they're letting you do this! I'm going to tell Clarice. I'll complain. This is insane. They have to stop. Is Ms. Robertson behind it? I'll have her fired!"

"Okay," she says, and I can tell from the sound of her voice that her head is turned away from me and toward the window. "You talk to Clarice. I'm sure that'll fix it."

"Did you tell them you don't want to do it?"

Her arm moves up as she shrugs. "Yeah. They said it wasn't optional. Could come in handy someday. They always blabber on about how they tailor our educations to what we'll need. Maybe I'll need to be good in a knife fight."

"You are never going to be in a knife fight," I say. My head is spinning. I don't know what's going on or why she hid this from me. But I'll tell Clarice, and Clarice will make sure whoever is responsible for this is in serious trouble.

I clutch Fia's hand, feeling the sand beneath my toes. I thought today would be magical, but as I match up what I saw with what I feel and hear and smell, I just keep seeing the expression on Fia's face from the vision.

She wasn't happy.

Nothing about her was happy. I remember my parents' faces, I remember what happy looks like, of course I do. The dozen other girls shout and laugh around us; I hear a few running through the shallow waves even though it's far too cold to get in.

We spent the afternoon at the aquarium. Eden could tell I was distracted and kept telling me the names of the weirdest fish, but I couldn't stop wondering about what's going on with Fia. Still can't. Fia pushes my hair aside where it's blown into my face and I try to smile at her.

"It's beautiful, isn't it?" I ask, hopeful.

"Yeah."

"Eden?" Clarice asks. "Could you take Annabelle's hand? I need to borrow Sofia for a minute."

I relax a little. I talked to Clarice yesterday and she was horrified. She said some of the trainers they brought on were new and overzealous, and what they were doing with Fia was completely inappropriate. She said she'd fix it immediately. I smile and let go of my sister's hand. Clarice is going to tell her that she'll never have to do that insane class again.

There's so much noise here, so many different sounds to filter through. The water, constant, under and over everything. Birds. I didn't notice the birds in my vision—I'll have to pay closer attention next time. Traffic. We must still be near a road. Conversations around me. I can pick out Clarice and Fia.

"Why?" Fia asks.

"We want to see if you can do it. Think of it as a game."

"It's stupid. I won't do it."

"You want out of Ms. Roberston's sessions?"

Pause. "Yes."

"Then show me you can do this. Focus. Go on instinct. All you need to do is figure out a way to get this into that woman's bag without anyone around her noticing."

Pause. "That's all?"

"That's all."

"It doesn't feel right."

"*Make* it feel right then. You can focus it. I know you can."

"Fine. Whatever."

Then the conversation is over and I'm confused. That wasn't what Clarice was going to talk to her about. Maybe Ms. Robertson is in charge of the self-defense classes. But what was that about a woman and a bag?

I let go of Eden's hand and sit where I am, sifting sand between my fingers, wondering if this is the part where Fia turns back with that look on her face.

"I'm gonna go down to the water; wanna come?" Eden asks, but I shake my head, lost in what I saw. She puts her hand on top of my hair. "You worry too much. Shout if you want me."

A few minutes later someone flops to the sand next to me, and I can tell from the scent and feel of her nearby that it's Fia.

"What did Clarice want?"

"Nothing. Just a stupid game."

"But you're out of the classes, right?"

"Right."

"Good." I smile and lean my head onto her shoulder. "I like how it smells out here."

"It smells like rotten things. You're crazy."

"It smells like it looks. And I know how it looks, too." I smile like the crazy person Fia said I was, and she lets out a small laugh, even though I can feel from the tension in her shoulder she still isn't happy. I'll make her happy. I can fix things. I can be the big sister. "Oh! They said the doctor should have some of the test results back soon, but they want some samples of your DNA to compare and—"

A crack louder than thunder rips through the air, and a flash of heat whooshes past, carrying stinging bits of sand. Fia knocks us to the ground, throwing herself on top of me, and everyone is screaming and I didn't see this, what happened, what happened?

"What happened?" I shout in Fia's ear. But then she shoves off me and she is gone in the blackness now, screaming, screaming as loud as she can.

"WHAT DID YOU MAKE ME DO? WHAT DID YOU DO? WHAT DID I DO?"

She screams and screams until a soft thud hits the ground

near me and then she is silent but everyone else is screaming and this is not the beach I saw and I crawl desperately in the sand, searching, because I don't know where Fia is.

Where is Fia?

FIA
Monday Evening
〜

"DRUGS, DRUGS, PLEASE GIVE ME DRUGS." I MAKE A face at my pale reflection. My arm hurts. My head hurts. I don't understand anything that's happened today. Annie put the hit on Adam. She's *helping* Keane. Why? And thanks to Keane's rules, I can't visit her or even call her without being spied on. How could she do this to me? To us? She *used* me.

My arm hurts.

My life hurts.

"Drugs, drugs, drugs, I want some drugs," I sing, dancing out of the bathroom and into my living room. It's a beautiful apartment, Lincoln Park, impeccably furnished. James picked it for me when we got back from Europe and they decided it was dangerous for me to have easy access to Annie. One too many stray thoughts of grabbing her and running. Stupid Readers.

So she stays at the school and I get "freedom" that is as much a prison as Annie's secure hall because they know I'll never leave her.

As long as I do exactly what I am told I am perfectly free.

"Drugs, James, drugs, drugs—" I stop short, almost tripping, and let my anger (always on simmer, I keep it on simmer just for this) explode. "What are *they* doing here?"

Ms. Robertson and Eden are sitting on my couch—*my couch*—and James is by the window on his phone. Anger, anger, anger, Eden is already squirming, looking like she's going to be sick. I turn to Ms. Robertson and mentally list every dirty, foul, obscene word I've ever heard or read. I start screaming them in my head, letting them bounce around inside my skull, the whole place a vast echo chamber of filth and bile and words, words, words.

Then, because her severe mouth is a single straight line but she hasn't gotten truly angry yet, I smile, bare all my teeth at her, and think three simple words: *Andy, Ashley, Ally.* She gasps in horror and rushes from the couch straight at me, grabbing both my arms (my arm, my arm, pain pain pain) and slamming me into the wall.

"How do you know their names? How?"

Andy, Ashley, Ally. Andy, Ashley, Ally. ANDY, ASHLEY, ALLY.

"STOP IT!" she screams, and I sigh in relief as James pulls her off me. Oh, my arm; spots dance in front of my eyes, but it's worth it.

Ms. Robertson is screaming at James and he's talking, trying to calm her down. I sink along the wall to the floor and laugh. I knew it was a good idea to pick up her cell phone when she left it out on her desk the other day. I didn't even have to sing pop songs, and my thoughts are safe.

"If she doesn't have anything to hide, then why does she do that? You don't know what it's like, having to listen in on her thoughts! She's a monster!"

"*Rawr*," I say.

James walks her to the door. "I think everyone could use a break. Doris, thank you so much for your efforts, and I promise your family is safe and she doesn't know where they are and even if she did"—he cuts a sharp glance my direction with his warm brown beautiful eyes—"she would never hurt them. She's just disoriented and in pain. It'll pass."

"I doubt that." She opens the door.

"Give my love to the kids," I shout as the door closes, and I've never seen that shade of red on a face. It's quite lovely, actually, I should aim for it more often.

Eden stands. Oh, Eden, why haven't you gotten out of here yet? You could go, you could be free—why are you still working with them? They have nothing on you.

"She's calming down," she says, "but her arm hurts a lot and she's very confused and angry. The last one goes without saying. She's not going to kill herself, though. Can I leave now? I have a headache."

James nods and I see the way she leans toward him, the hand she casually puts on his arm, before pulling herself back and walking carefully to the door. She is aware of how her hips look in those jeans—she wants him to want her. I wonder if he still does. I send a big burst of anger in her direction as a parting gift. I hate her.

"Fia," James says, raising an eyebrow. His hair is somewhere between blond and brown, golden really, backlit by the last rays of sun sneaking through my huge picture window, and he is glowing and so very, very handsome. I'm glad Ms. Robertson is gone because I'm thinking things about James I don't want her to hear. About tracing the broad line of his shoulders and his arms, about the way he walks. The curve of his lips. I'm thinking about running my hand down his stomach. He knows what my hands do, he knows about them. He'd still let me, I bet.

I wonder if Adam would let me touch him with my horrible hands, if he knew, if he really knew. I told him I killed people, but I don't think he understands what that means. He can't. If he could, he wouldn't be Adam. Calm and steady and sweet. I wonder where he is, if he's okay.

Don't think about it. Thoughts aren't safe, ever.

James is staring back at me. He knows he's handsome. He uses it to his advantage constantly. Is it bad that I like that about him? I miss him so much. I miss how easy it was, being his.

"James," I say, mimicking his tone, then stand and stumble over to the couch, throwing myself across it. Dr. Grant stitched me up all nice, then James brought me home and actually let me take something. They never let me take anything. (It'll mess with my abilities, they say. You'll take too many again, they don't say.) "I would like some more drugs, please."

"I think no."

"Why not? Come on. I earned it. Besides, I'm about to start my period, and you know how PMSing messes with everything." I beam at him, but he doesn't so much as squirm.

"I seem to recall Clarice saying you were actually at your best then—you just couldn't focus your intuition on what we needed you to do, only on what you wanted to do."

"Yes, well, I seem to recall Clarice being dead."

"Fia," he says, and it's like a sigh. He sits on the other end of the couch and puts my feet across his lap. I shouldn't let him touch me. I don't, usually, because he is a liar and I promised Annie, I promised her so long ago. I broke that promise in Europe, I wanted to break it completely, but I learned better.

But Annie.

Annie.

Annie wanted me to kill Adam.

She wanted me to close gray eyes and put long, soft, sure fingers under the ground. How could she want him dead? Did she want *me* to do it? How could she set me up for that?

I don't know her at all. All these years, all these things I've done, all these things I've become to keep her happy, to keep her safe. I don't know her. I tap tap tap Annie's betrayal onto my leg.

"Listen," James says, and he's rubbing my feet. His hands engulf them—he's tall, so tall, and stronger than me by far. Right now he could take me in a fight, I think. Maybe not. He wears contacts. I could use that to my advantage.

His fingers linger at my ankle. I haven't let him touch me since I made him bring me back to Chicago. I think it's actually affecting him. Maybe there are a lot of other things I could use to my advantage against James. "What am I supposed to listen to?" I turn and look up at him through my eyelashes.

"You need to calm down. Quit antagonizing the other women. It makes my job a lot harder."

"Oh, poor dear. You have a hard job? I can't imagine."

He yanks my pinky toe. "I think you have a very good imagination. They complain to my father, and then my father suspects I'm not doing a good job managing here." His voice gets tight. Daddy issues. I wish I had daddy issues. Though I suppose I have issues with *his* daddy. "And if I'm not your manager, I can't help you anymore."

I sit up and pull my feet away from him. I look straight in his eyes. I do not look away and I do not let him look away. "I got shot and I killed someone. Do you have any idea—" I let my voice break. It's not hard. "Do you have any idea what that feels like? What it does to me? How are you *helping* me?"

"I want to. I'm trying to. But, see, that," he says, cupping the side of my face with his warm hand. "Why can't you let them see that? That's a perfectly acceptable reaction. That's a reaction they can report without getting us in trouble. That's a reaction that gets you trusted in this system."

I shove his hand away and stand. "I'd hate for you to get in any trouble." I put my hands on my hips. "I want something to help me sleep."

His phone rings and when he looks at the screen, his face shifts, gets harder and further away. Must be Daddy Dearest. He answers it.

No, no, no. This could take all night. How can I ever get to sleep now? I grab my own phone and call Annie, walking back into the hall, away from James. Annie answers. I need to talk to her, need her to explain.

But she can't right now, not without revealing that I didn't kill Adam. They're always listening.

"Fia? How are you feeling? Are you okay?"

"Oh, I'm peachy! Never been better. I wanted to talk to you

about something you said earlier."

There's a long pause, as she tries to feel out whether or not she can talk around it without giving us away. "You mean my vision?"

"Yup. Your vision."

Another long silence. "I don't think you should go dancing, is all. It'll make sense later, I promise. Please trust me. When I can explain, it will make sense."

I grit my teeth, adding the pain in my jaw to the pain in my head and my arm and my heart. "Sure. Everything does. Later. Too late, actually. You know, I don't think you understand what you're asking of me. Do you have *any idea* what you're asking of me?"

"Please, Fia. Please. I'm so sorry. I didn't mean for this to happen. I didn't want it to happen to you. We'll talk about it. I promise."

"No. It's fine. Fine, fine, fine. Everyone uses me, everyone bosses me around. Guess you finally caught on." I remember what we're allegedly talking about for whoever is listening. "But the funny thing is, I wouldn't even have considered going dancing tonight if you hadn't brought it up. What's that term? Self-fulfilling prophecy?"

"That's not funny."

"I think it's hilarious. Let me know if I have to kill anyone tomorrow, okay? Bye!" I end the call, then throw my phone against the wall. She's—I can't process this. I can't deal with it. If she's the one who wanted the hit, she would have had to convince Keane that Adam needed to die. Why? Why would she? Even if she didn't make me go, she's still the reason I had to.

She has to remember. She can't have forgotten what it was like before Clarice. What it's been like ever since. But no. She used me, just like Keane, just like everyone else. And I screwed up, again, always, and now she's in danger and she didn't want me to not kill him. How could she be disappointed in me for making the right choice for the first time in years?

Annie. Annie. Annabelle. Anna*hell*. I stomp into my room and pull all the clothes out of my closet, throwing them behind me, until I find the perfect strapless black dress. It'd probably be more accurate to call it a dressless black strap. I laugh.

I wish Annie could have heard that joke.

Sharp red stilettos. I don't know why I need the sharp ones, but they're right for tonight. I can't do my hair one-handed; it's falling in waves down my back. Twist a strand back from my face. Dark eye makeup to better match my Cameron Underhill ID. Cameron is twenty-two.

I'm twenty-two tonight.

The only thing ruining the effect is the bandage on my left arm (it joins my other faint scars), but nothing to be done there. Shot is shot is shot. No room for a knife in this dress. I lean back and ponder. Don't need one tonight.

I slink down the hall into the main room.

James is standing by the window, the sun now set, his beautiful, strong, all-American-boy face creased and pinched. "We need to be more careful. This type of work isn't good for her. It risks everything I've built up the last two years. Why don't we have her back on stocks and trading and espionage? She's perfect there. This—" he pauses, only for a second but I know his dad will see the weakness there "—assassination work messes her up. She won't be useful for months in this state of mind."

Oh, useful. I won't be *useful*. Heaven forbid. If they only knew what their pet had done. A pause, where I can only guess what the elder Keane is saying. I've never met him. None of the girls from the school ever have. I tap tap tap. Tap tap tap. I need to get out of here.

I grab my purse from the counter by the door, take off my heels, and hook them around my wrist.

"Yes, sir. I understand." James's dad can't see the way his jaw tightens, the way every muscle in his body traces a line of anger and barely controlled rebellion. He is never more beautiful to me than when he is livid. But still James does as James is told. Good boy, James. Have another treat. Sit, James. Roll over. Play dead. Kill. There's a good son!

"Going out," I call, and he whips around in time to see me

blow a kiss before I slam the door shut and sprint down the stairs, past the bewildered doorman, and out of the building. I can't run away. But I can run.

And I can dance.

FIA
Two-and-a-Half Years Ago
~

ANNIE WANTS ME TO MOVE BACK INTO HER ROOM.

She doesn't understand. I can't. I can't live with her because I can't tell her, and if I live with her, she'll know, she'll figure it out. She's worried about me.

She has no idea.

I am a murderer.

That day on the beach. I am trapped in that day on the beach. I take the small package. It fits in the palm of my hand. I focus on getting it in the woman's bag without being seen. It's easy. I know exactly what to do. No one notices a thing out of place, as the gangly teenage girl chases her ball past with a determined look.

No one connects her to the explosion that kills two people

three minutes later.

Her. Me. Her. Me. I did that.

"Please choose, Sofia." Clarice is sitting in front of me, calm and placid. She is always calm—I want to claw her eyes out sometimes. On the table between us are five boxes wrapped in plain brown paper. Five boxes. Two people. One explosion. Two murderers in this room.

I can't leave now, not ever. I'd get caught. They'd know. They'd know it was me. I can't tell anyone what this school really is because then I'd have to tell them what I did.

"Who cares. They're all boxes. Why does it matter which box I choose?"

"We need to test the limits. Can you make the correct choices on instinct only when you understand what is going on, or can your intuitive senses help you make the correct choices even when you have no idea what you are choosing?"

"If a tree falls in the forest and no one is around, does anyone give a crap?" I mutter.

"Now, please."

I glare at her. We are murderers together, Clarice and me. I point to the box on the far left. "I'd take that one."

She smiles. "Very good."

"What's in them?"

"It doesn't matter."

"Of course it doesn't." I lean back in my chair and stare at the ceiling. "Can I be done now?"

"It's interesting," she says, carefully picking up the boxes and stacking them in the corner of the big, cinder-block walled, windowless basement room. Annie has never been down here. Most of the girls haven't. Only Eden and I are left from my original class, anyway. "I have the hardest time seeing you. Some people are easier than others, of course, but your constant ability to react without thinking makes it very, very hard to see anything in your future."

I wonder if she could still have visions with her eyes clawed out. Annie loves her. Annie thinks she's the best thing that ever happened to us. Annie needs her. They are running tests and diagnostics, and every three months there is another bit of hope for Annie's sight.

I can't leave anyway because I am a murderer and they would send me to jail and I couldn't take care of Annie if I were in jail.

"Did you know we had no idea you existed?" She walks over to the door and taps on it three times. Tap tap goes my finger. Two taps. Two lives. "It was only Annie we were interested in. She's proved less than exceptional, but you were the real find. At first we thought you were a Reader, or maybe a Feeler, since you knew this school wasn't all it was set up to be. But you've proved far more interesting than any of that."

"Goodie for me." I could pick up the chair. I could smash it into her face. I wonder if I'm going to. Would she have already seen it if I was going to? Guess I'm not going to, then. Or she just can't see it. I'm bored. I want to go sleep.

Sleep, sleep.

Tap tap. I don't know what their faces looked like. I never really saw them. Would knowing what their faces looked like make the nightmares better or worse? I know their names. I looked up the story online, later, much later.

I killed a senator. Does that make it murder and treason? I'm scared. I'm scared in here, and I'm scared out there. I can never leave.

The door opens and three men dressed in gray sweats come in. They each have a small black thing in their hands, like a boxy cell phone. I don't know what it is, but every sense is on alert and my heart is racing and my focus is narrowing, getting sharper. This is bad. I need to get out of this room. I stand and put the table between us, gripping Clarice's chair. It's heavy. Too heavy for much, I wish it were lighter, but I can take out someone's leg.

Why do I need to take out someone's leg?

"Sofia, these gentlemen are going to help you with some training. They've all got stun guns. Your job is to get out of the room."

"Without getting shocked?" I stare at her, aghast. We haven't done one of these in so long. I thought we were done.

"No. Your job is to fight back and get out of the room in

spite of getting shocked." She smiles pleasantly. "Consider it an exercise in focusing through pain."

I should have smashed her head in with the chair, seen how well she could focus then.

Don't cry, don't cry. Annie can hear if I'm crying. She can't see me curled in a ball on the couch, every part of my body in pain. She can't see that I'm biting my wrist as hard as I can. I got out of the room. Oh, it hurts so much.

"So, what's new?" she asks. She sounds nervous. She should be. She hasn't tried to touch me today.

"Nothing."

"You haven't been here much."

"Busy. School stuff."

"Oh." There's a long pause and I hope she is done trying to talk to me. "I've been getting better. That's good, right?"

"Better at what?"

"Seeing things. Clarice thought I should focus on you, and it helps. A little. But lately I haven't been seeing things exactly how they will happen. I've been seeing . . . I don't know. Bits and pieces that feel like they mean something more. Like maybe they're still shifting and not set. It feels . . . big. Not like what I used to see, where it was something that really was going to happen exactly like that, and I only had to figure out how to understand the images. These visions are more like puzzles.

Lots of little pieces. Like a recent vision, there was a guy with light hair and one with dark hair, opposite each other like they were two sides of a mirror. And a flash of you, and one of Clarice, and the color red, and a room all filled with tables and chairs but really fancy looking, official . . . I don't know. It's kind of scary, and I don't understand it yet. But some are good. I've even started dreaming them. Sometimes they're happy." She gets a sort of dreamy smile on her face.

I sit up (it hurts, it hurts, my body hurts) and grab her hand in mine. She startles; I haven't been touching her at all lately. I don't like my hands anymore. I used to think they were pretty. Now they look like they belong on someone else's body. Someone who kills people. "Listen to me. Do *not* tell them. Don't tell them you're seeing more. Don't tell Clarice. Don't even think about what you're seeing."

"Why? Fia, you're scaring me. Why won't you tell me what's going on?"

"Promise me you won't tell them!"

"I won't! I promise! What's going on?"

I drop her hand. "Nothing. And stop trying to see me. You won't like it." I walk out of her dorm room.

Down the hall.

Down the stairs.

Doesn't matter where I go.

Outside the entrance hall I nearly bump into a boy. He's

wearing a coat and he is tall and he belongs black-and-white and shirtless on the wall of a clothing store and his warm brown eyes are completely glazed over. I simultaneously want to kiss him and to get as far away from him as possible. He feels wrong, he feels dangerous; my heart speeds up the same way for him that it did for the stun guns.

Everything here feels wrong all the time. But he feels exciting wrong.

"Hey," he says, grinning, his eyes tracing over me without apology.

"Hey." There are no boys here. Not teenagers, anyway. Only men. With weapons. (It hurts, it hurts, my body hurts.)

"James. Keane. James Keane." He sticks out his hand for me to shake it.

I keep my murderer hands to myself. "Keane as in the Keane Foundation?"

"The very same!"

"I should bash your brains in right now," I say, but I am too tired to do it.

"You're the third person to say that to me today!" He winks, then takes my arm and links it through his own. "Why don't you take me on the grand tour of the secret school."

"Why don't you take a walking tour through rush-hour traffic?"

He laughs. "I like you. What did you say your name is?"

"Sofia."

"Sofia. Soooofia. Sofia, I have done something very bad."

It is wrong to go with him as he pulls me down the hall toward the empty classrooms. I go anyway. "I'll bet I've done something worse." Tap tap goes my finger.

"I would love to hear it if you have. But I get to go first. I have"—he looks both ways down the hall in exaggerated caution, then leans in and whispers right in my ear (wrong, wrong, but it doesn't stop the shivers from going up and down my spine; he is gorgeous, I have never been this close to a gorgeous boy) —"broken into a boarding school for special teenage girls."

I shove him back, glare. "That's it? That's pathetic."

"It's not! It's very, very bad. You see, I brought whiskey with me. *Stolen* whiskey."

I yawn, patting my hand over my mouth.

"Stolen from the dean of my college."

I check the watch I am not wearing for the time.

"After he expelled me."

I look him straight in the eyes. "I delivered a package bomb that killed two people."

His face freezes. I shouldn't have told. I shouldn't have. I don't care. I stare defiantly at him.

His frozen face melts into a smile. "Well, my dear girl, you win. I think this calls for a drink." He tries to open the nearest door, but it's locked. He takes a step back, lifts his leg, and kicks it open with a resounding crack. "That'll hurt in the morning. Ladies first." He holds out a hand to the now-open room.

He doesn't care that I killed two people.

What is wrong with him?

I walk in. (In this room I have picked which gun was unloaded out of ten options. And then they pulled the trigger on me. I have picked stocks that went on to skyrocket. I have picked which pencil I would shove into Ms. Robertson's ear until she kicked me out for thinking about it.)

James staggers/swaggers past me and sits on the floor against the wall out of view of the damaged door. He pats the floor next to him.

I sit. He passes me a bottle he pulls out of his coat and I know—I know, I know—I should not ever taste alcohol.

I take a swig.

I choke and cough and he laughs. I take another and manage to swallow it.

"That's a girl. Now, do you want to know a secret?"

"I know too many secrets."

"Well, you don't know any of mine. My mother was psychic. Genuine, see-the-future, real-deal psychic." He waits. "You aren't impressed?"

"Should I be?"

"Probably not. Made it awfully hard to really get into trouble, though. She could always see it coming. Do you want to know the trick to getting in trouble under the watchful eye of a psychic?"

I think of the nailed-shut windows. I think of Clarice. I think of the two, the two, the two who are now zero. Tap tap. "Yes."

"Don't plan it. Don't even think about it. The second you get an inkling of what you could do, do it then. Never plan anything ahead of time. Always go on pure instinct."

I smile, take another long drink before he pulls it away. "I can do that."

"To my mother," he says, raising the bottle. "And to yours." He passes it back to me.

"Mine's dead."

"Mine, too!"

He doesn't seem sorry. Usually people are sorry about dead parents. I like that he isn't sorry. "Both my parents died in a car wreck. My sister saw it before it happened. It still happened."

"My mother shot herself in the head. Yesterday."

I stare at him in shock and horror. Then I hand the bottle back and say, "Well, my dear boy, you win. This calls for a drink."

He laughs, and I do too, and I realize it's the first time I've laughed in six months. I think I'm in love with him. And I know I'm in love with this drink and the soft, fuzzy way it makes me feel.

"I broke in here tonight to see the reason my mother blew her brains out. I'm very disappointed it's just a building. I'm less disappointed in the company."

"I would burn this school to the ground if I could."

"You'd be hurting the wrong people. It's my father. You should burn him. I hate him."

"To your father." I take another few gulps.

"To burning my father to the ground."

In the morning when they find us passed out next to each other on the floor, James is sent away but not before he salutes me. Clarice doesn't say a word about it, but Annie is in a rage when I get back to my room.

My head hurts, hurts. I remember the laughing, though. And his face. And that he knows what I did and he still sat next to me and laughed and told me I had the prettiest eyes he'd ever seen but that I was far too young for him to kiss until he had had at least three more drinks.

I don't know why Annie is talking so loud. Why is she talking? I want her to stop talking.

"Listen to me, Fia!" She grabs my shoulders and forces me to look into her face, even though she can't see mine. I stick my tongue out at her. "Never drink again."

"But it was fun," I whine.

"Anything could have happened to you!"

My head agrees. She's right, I know she's right. "Fine."

"And stay away from James."

"Why? What does it matter? He's gone. I'll probably never see him again." I want to, though. He was wrong, but it didn't make me feel sick—it made me feel dizzy, that feeling you get on the edge of a very high place where you feel immortal and fragile at the same time, and I liked it.

"I promised you I wouldn't tell Clarice about the new things I was seeing. You promise me you'll stay away from James. He's bad news; he's dangerous, Fia."

Not as dangerous as I am, Annie. I promise her anyway.

ANNIE
Monday Evening
~

"I NEED TO TALK TO MR. KEANE. NOW." I TAP MY FOOT impatiently at Hallway Darren, who smells of mustard. I've tried to call Fia back, but it goes straight to voice mail. She's going to do something stupid; I know she's going to go dancing. Probably right now. She can't mess up, not again. I'm getting so much better. I know I'll see what we need soon, something that will get us free. Something that will atone for all the ways I've destroyed my sister.

I can feel it—it's close, that future where we're free. That secret future I've never told anyone about, that I don't even know any details about other than the way I *feel* in it. I have to get things back under control so we can find that future.

Darren shifts in his chair. It creaks. "I'll call his secretary and see if I can set something up."

"You might want to mention I've seen his death. His immi-
nent death. Just so they know who to blame when he doesn't get
warned in time."

I've read of the blood draining from people's faces when
they're scared. I like to imagine that's what's happening to Darren right now. I hear something thud to the floor—small, must
be his phone, butterfingers—before he stammers to someone
that I need an appointment with Mr. Keane immediately. He
doesn't say why. Probably doesn't want to be culpable if something really does go wrong.

"He's in the building." Darren says, relief evident in his voice.
No one knows where Keane will be at any given time, and he's
very rarely here. This is lucky. "I can take you up right now."

"There's a good boy."

He tries to take my elbow. He always tries to take my elbow.
I want to take my elbow to his face. Instead, I move it away and
walk down the hall to the elevator on my own. As if I don't
know the confines of my prison. As if I am not aware of every
square foot of space that holds me here, where no one can get to
me and where no one can get me out. These walls hold Fia, too,
even though she's not in them.

I wish she could leave me. But I know she never will.

The elevator's familiar hum and cheerful ding announce our
arrival on the top floor. I've only been here one other time, just

last week. It smells clean, perfectly clean, the air purified and washed and dried of everything that goes on underneath it. The rest of the school and dorms smell like women. This floor has not a single scent of perfume or floral shampoo or lotion.

I am the only woman here who Keane will see. I suppose I should be flattered, but he knows I'm the only one who can see him without *seeing* him. He won't let Readers or Feelers within two floors of himself, and he never lets any of the psychics see his face, because if we don't know his face, we can't recognize him if we see him in a vision.

A bit paranoid, our mysterious boss. Probably comes with the territory when you have US senators killed. Fia still doesn't know she told me about that. Oh, Fia.

Good thing Darren isn't bright enough to have figured out that there's no way I could have seen a vision with Keane in it and known what I was seeing. I step away from the elevator doors. Then I stand. And wait. It's humiliating. I try to stand as straight as possible, to keep my face perfectly even and composed. I have been living on my few prison floors for so long that being anywhere else without Eden terrifies me. It could all be open. It could stretch on forever without any walls. It could be nothing but an infinite white space.

I don't know. I can never know. And I can't do a thing until someone lets me. I miss the way Fia used to hold my hand. I felt like I lost a limb when she stopped doing it.

"This way, Miss Rosen."

I startle. Someone is right next to me. The carpet up here is so thick, I didn't even hear him approach. But I know his voice. He is—Daniel. John. Daniel/John. The man who recognized that Fia belonged here, too. Without him, it would have only been me, it would have only ever been me.

"Daniel. Or was it John?"

"You have an excellent memory." He takes my elbow lightly and leads me to my left. I count the steps. Thirty-two until he directs me to go ahead of him and the carpet changes. It's a different room this time.

The door closes behind me. He didn't escort me to a chair. I wish I could kill him.

I know Keane is in the room. I can feel him like electricity, but he doesn't say anything. So I walk forward, shoulders back, one hand lifted casually in front of myself. What if there is no chair or desk? What if I walk until I run into Keane? The idea of touching him makes me want to turn and run. I stop, and stand where I am.

"Good evening, Annabelle." His voice is deep and even and devoid of tone.

"I need to know who shot my sister." I wait. He says nothing. "I didn't see them. It's hard to see Sofia when she's out and acting on pure instinct. She shifts, based on things that don't make sense, things that shouldn't affect anything, so we—I—can't see it. I only get glimpses, and even those don't always happen. So I need to know who else was there and whether they were there for her or Adam Denting. If they were there for Denting, then we have no more problems because he's dead. But if they were there for Sofia, that means you aren't the only one using psychics, which means our problems are very, very big."

He lets out a considering breath. It is the first noise he's made aside from his greeting. He does not move. He does not fidget. He is not a person in my head. He is a robot, chrome and steel, without blood, without a heart. I cannot even begin to piece together in my head what this soulless voice should look like.

"You are very bright, Annabelle. Did you know what Adam Denting was working on?"

I do not let so much as a muscle in my face twitch. I knew only what his work would lead to. "I have no idea. It wasn't a real-life vision. I already told you—I just saw his name swallowing up yours, destroying it."

"You're seeing in the abstract now. I find that very intriguing. You will, of course, keep us posted on any more of these idea visions."

I hate that I had to admit I can see more than just the solid future after promising Fia I never would. But what I really saw—face after face after face of women, women who I *knew* could see and feel and read, suddenly coming into focus and then fading into black, with a voice that sounded like my own whispering Adam Denting's name over and over again . . . I panicked. I had to help those women, keep them safe.

"Of course," I snap. "It would help if I knew what anyone actually does here, though." I still don't. All these years later, everything Fia's done.

I have no idea what any of it is for.

I am so stupid. After the vision about Adam, I demanded a meeting with Keane and told him the first thing I could think of to get him to order a hit immediately. Oh, Fia, I didn't want you to have to kill anyone, ever. I never thought they'd send you, but I needed Adam Denting dead.

We all did.

I wonder how Keane is sitting. What his chair looks like. How he moves his hands. Apparently he's done with me, though. He says, "I'm looking into the disturbance. It isn't your concern."

"If it involves my sister, it is. You know no one can see her like I do. Are you really going to risk losing her?"

He won't. I know he won't. Of all of us, he's put the most time into her. With what she did two years ago, any of the rest of us would have been dead. Immediately. No questions. Fia got a pass.

"The name we have is Lerner. Whether that is a person or the entire group we don't know yet. They aren't playing on the same field as we are; however, they're getting close. We believe we have a few pictures of their people, but those won't do you any good, now, will they?"

I bristle. I think I hear a ghost of a laugh.

"Rest assured that I have nothing but your sister's best interests at heart, as I do with all my girls. And you know that *your* best interest is to keep your sister working."

"How could I forget. I'll look for anything with Lerner."

"Give your sister my regards."

I turn and walk out, knowing exactly how many steps will take me away from that monster. Once again wishing I were Fia, Fia who could have killed him with her bare hands.

Fia who is impossibly broken because she can do just that.

Back at my own table, a mug of tea between my hands, I can finally breathe again. I know where I am in space. It's not where I want to be, but at least I know it.

I bring the mug to my face to blink in the steam. Lerner. I'll bet anything they were there for Adam. No one could track Fia's movements that well. Not even Clarice could have.

It's so wrong that I miss her sometimes. I know it's wrong. I can't help it.

I breathe in again, deeper, and light bursts in front of my eyes. I can see! The familiar euphoria fills me like the steam from my tea, expanding in my lungs. And then I process what I'm seeing.

A guy sitting at a table under a bright light. He has the long arms and long legs and nice eyes that Fia told me about.

He can only be Adam Denting. She was right. I do like him. I ordered him dead, but I like him. I like his messy hair and kind eyes. I even like his ears.

He's fidgeting, looking down and up and over his shoulder. He's scared. Someone is talking to him. He's nervously answering questions about who he is and what his research is, questions about who Sofia Rosen is and exactly what she told him about herself.

And a woman's voice, from somewhere I can't see, reassures him that he's safe now that he's with Lerner.

ANNIE

Two Years Ago

~

FIA'S IN MY ROOM. SHE'S BEEN AVOIDING ME FOR SO long, but lately she's here all the time. It makes me happy.

And sad. Because it's different. She's quiet. She never laughs. I wish she could laugh and that it could be easy between us, that Eden could still come over when Fia's here and we could all three just hang out.

I'm using the braille display on my new laptop. I've had speech-to-text technology for a while, but this way I can read everything instead of waiting for the computer to read it for me. This is one of the things I tried to get the public school system to bring in, but they never had the budget to aid one blind student. Now all I have to do is find the products and technology I want to try, tell Clarice about them, and within a week they're here.

My fingers fly through websites for research on my senior project, an examination of adaptations of the Cassandra myth from ancient Greece. "This display is freaky cool, Fia."

"Mmmm hmmm."

"You doing homework?"

"Nope."

"What are you doing?"

"Wondering if a fourteen-year-old who is an accessory to murder can be tried as an adult."

My fingers stop midword. "What? Why would you wonder about that?"

"Just something to think about. It seems like for most crimes you won't get tried as an adult, but murder they push the age pretty low."

I frown. "Is this for a class?" Only Eden is left from her age group. Girls leave the school a lot for other programs run by the foundation or get kicked out because the curriculum isn't working for them. I'm so relieved it's never happened to us. Aunt Ellen hasn't even written in two years. I worry about Fia getting kicked out—I literally have no idea what we'd do.

"Oh, I never go to class. Why would I go to class?"

I knock the braille display over as I whip around to face her. "You aren't going to class?"

"Class comes to me. I read a lot. I sleep a lot. Nobody cares."

"That's terrible! I can't believe this. What kind of curriculum do they have you on? I understand that they're flexible, but that's unacceptable." I pause, not wanting to ask, needing to ask. "Are they . . . are you doing those weird self-defense things again?"

"Mostly running and strength training. You never know when you'll need to sprint three miles. Besides, we're focused more on breaking and entering now."

"That's not funny."

"It really isn't, is it?"

I stand and walk over to my bed, feel for her. Her head is hanging off the edge, upside down. Her hair has gotten long, longer than it was when I saw her in the vision on the beach. I wonder how else she's changed.

"You aren't happy, are you?" I'd been hoping she'd adapt, that whatever weird things were going on with her, whatever strange dynamic she had here would change. I swallow hard. I am a terrible person. I know she's not happy. She hasn't been happy in months. Years. But I kept waiting and hoping. Not because I thought she'd change. Because *I* needed her to be happy so I could keep being happy here.

Fia doesn't sound upset when she finally speaks. She sounds far away. "I don't even remember what happy felt like. I think it probably felt like that night I got really drunk with James. Soft and fuzzy, everything spinning and out of focus."

I pull her up, pull her off the bed and onto my lap. She curls into me like a child, though she's as tall as I am now, she has to be, all arms and legs. She rests her head against my shoulder, and it's wet where her eyes are.

"Oh, Fia, Fia. I'm so sorry. I'm going to fix this." How could I let it get this bad? She's depressed. Obviously. There has to be something they can put her on, some sort of antidepressant, to make it better until we can figure out how to get her happy again. "I'm going to take care of you."

"You can't," she says, and her voice is hollow. "It's my job to take care of you."

I'm taken back to when I was seven and she was five. We were in our second house, the one without any stairs. I was putting together puzzles in the family room, feeling their contours to match the edges. When I finished I needed Fia to come in and tell me what the pictures were. But I was way better at puzzles than her; I always finished them first.

I heard the kitchen door slam. "What were you thinking?" My mother's voice, high and sharp and sweet, was shrill with panic. "Greg, call the doctor."

"She'll be okay." Dad's voice was warm. It made me think of blankets straight out of the dryer, sticky with static, thrown around our shoulders. I didn't remember much of what either of them looked like—just vague ideas of brown hair and long, long legs.

"She could have done permanent damage! Fia, sweetheart, you never stare straight at the sun! You could go blind!"

Fia's voice came out laced with tears. "I wanted to."

"You wanted to go blind?"

"So I could be like Annie. I want to be like Annie. You said you were getting her a dog."

"Oh, sweetheart. We won't get the dog for a long time. And you don't want to be blind. If you were blind, too, who would take care of Annie? It's your job to take care of her. You're very special. Usually big sisters are in charge of little sisters, but in our family it's the opposite. Can you do that? Can you take care of her?"

"I can! I will." Fia's little voice was solemn with the weight of responsibility.

I picked up my puzzle and pushed it, piece by piece, out the open window. I'd always thought I was there to help Fia. To calm her down when she got too angry, to comfort her when she got too sad, to tell her to shut up when she was being obnoxious.

After that she held my hand more. I let her. But I didn't look for ways to help her anymore. She was the special one, apparently.

"I'm sorry," I whisper now, running her hair through my fingers. "I've been so selfish. You know you don't have to take care of me, right? You don't have to worry about me. I'm not your responsibility. If you want to leave . . . " I swallow hard. I don't want to leave. I've even been thinking about going to college close by and asking Clarice if I can stay on as a sort of resident adviser, though more than half the girls we started with are gone now. Eden and I both want to stay. Her family is seriously screwed up—she lives at the school all the time, too, even holidays. We'll go to college together, in the city. Maybe I'll be a teacher here, after I get my degree. Help girls like Eden and me, help them understand themselves, know they aren't crazy.

I take a deep breath. "You can. You can leave, if you want to. We'll find Aunt Ellen. You don't have to feel bad. You don't have to stay at the school because of me." I reach down for her hand.

She rips it away like I've burned her, sits up, shoves herself off me. "I don't *have* to stay, huh? I don't have to stay? I'm only here because of you! This is your fault! All of it!"

I frown, hurt. "I didn't make you come!"

"It's your fault I'm all you have! You let Mom and Dad die! You saw what was going to happen. You SAW it. And you didn't stop it! If you hadn't let them die, we'd never be here in the first place! Everything would be okay! THIS IS ALL YOUR FAULT!"

Fia, who said she never blamed me, who promised me, *promised* me, had blamed me this whole time.

"Get out of my room," I say.

"Make me."

"GET OUT OF MY ROOM! GET OUT OF MY LIFE!"

The slamming door is my only response.

Later that night I can't sleep. I feel too guilty. I shouldn't have said those things to her. I'm the big sister. And she's hurting, has been for a long time. I need to help her. I need to be the calm one, the one who can be in control, see this for what it is.

She needs help.

I pad down the hall. I don't know if the lights are still on or not, but I know the way to Clarice's office by heart. She works late a lot; maybe she'll still be there. It feels right to be doing something.

Voices are coming from her office. The door must be open. I walk closer, then stop. At least I know she's awake. I'll wait in the hall until she's done.

I'm about to sit when I hear Fia's name.

"Surely there has to be a better way to control her." Ms. Robertson's voice.

"Eden says she's getting worse. The guilt is fading and being replaced by anger and something Eden calls a swirling mess of empty despair. That girl has a thing or two to learn about precise definitions." I don't know whose voice that is; it sounds vaguely familiar, but I'm sure I've never had instruction from her. Almost all my classes are with Clarice, one-on-one.

"It's an unusual case." Clarice. So Clarice knows Fia's struggling, too, and she's already working with the rest of the faculty to help. I smile. "The other girls worth keeping are easy enough. By the time they put it all together, they're in so deep and enjoy the perks so much they don't realize it wasn't their own idea. Like Eden. Broken homes are wonderful, aren't they?" A smattering of laughter. I don't like the feeling of this conversation.

Clarice's voice is closer to the door. I shrink back against the wall, praying that the hall lights are off. I don't hear them. There's no hum. But I don't usually try to listen to the lights. Maybe I'm wrong. Maybe they can see me right now. Maybe they're standing there, silently laughing at me. Mrs. Robertson needs to see you to read you. Can she see me? I slide a few feet back toward the hall to the stairs.

"But it's different with Sofia," Clarice says. "It always has been. There was no way to gain her trust and then build up to what we wanted her to do. She knew from the very beginning she didn't want to be here or do what we want her to, so it's been a fight all along."

The unknown voice who talked about Eden: "The guilt is fading, though. You'll have to figure out a new method to keep her from running."

Clarice, in a tone so matter-of-fact my blood runs cold: "I already know exactly when she's going to try. We'll have something in place by then. She's the school's top priority; Keane is deeply invested in her. All the little empaths and Seers are replaceable. Sofia is special."

"She's a monster." Ms. Robertson.

Clarice, small laugh: "But she's *our* monster." Creaking. People getting up from chairs. I need to leave. I was not supposed to hear this. "And we'll keep doing whatever it takes so she stays ours."

I turn and run silently back down the hall. Whatever it takes, whatever it takes, whatever it takes. It echoes through my head. They'll *keep* doing whatever it takes. What else have they already done? It doesn't matter. I'm getting my sister out of here. I won't fail her anymore.

Tomorrow we run.

FIA
Monday Evening
~

I BRIEFLY CONSIDER STOPPING AT A LIBRARY TO CHECK for an email from Adam, but it doesn't feel right. Besides which, I don't want to. I don't want to think about Adam and the way he looked at me, the way I saw him decide to trust me. I don't want to think about how normal and safe it made me feel when he was driving. I don't want to think about things like normal and safe, things I can't have.

I don't want to do anything tonight, nothing at all, but spin and pulse and pound. My fingers cannot tap tap tap when I am dancing. Annie can't betray me while I'm dancing. James can't use me. I can't hear my own thoughts. I haven't been dancing in four months, not since we left Greece, and I ache for it.

I run a few blocks south, then cut in to the city. Not sure

where I'm going. I never plan ahead. Learned my lesson about that a long time ago. Thank you, beautiful James.

There, ahead of me, a line snaking around a sidewalk. The unmistakable thumping hum of bass that will push right through me. Perfect. I look up and choke on a laugh. The place is called Vision.

Of course it is.

It's too early for such a long line. Must be a celebrity DJ or something. I slip into my stilettos and walk straight up to the front. There, third person. A guy with carefully sculpted hair, even more carefully sculpted arms and pecs, a shirt picked especially to showcase them. Here with two friends, no girls.

"Hi," I say, reaching over the velvet rope to trace my hand along the edge of his shoulder. Oh, my hands, my hands make me shudder, but he doesn't shudder. "I hate lines." I smile at him, and I know that I am beautiful and beauty is a tool. It will get me what I want, and what I want is the front of this line.

"Hey." His eyes travel the length of my legs.

"Good thing I'm meeting you guys here so I don't have to wait in line, right?"

He smiles. His teeth are so white they would glow under a black light. "Good thing."

I duck under the rope and he puts his arm around my shoulder (don't touch my shoulder, it hurts), and I could break his arm, I know how to twist it just so to pop-pop-pop it right out of the socket, but he seems nice enough and that would get in the way of dancing.

He even pays my cover charge, the darling boy. Good thing, because I don't have cash after I gave it all to Adam and I don't want a card pinging my location. We walk in and I can't hear his voice, which is another good thing. He shouldn't have a voice. A body is fine, he is allowed to have a body. I need other bodies to dance around me so I can get lost.

This club is like any other club anywhere in the world. There's a waterfall and fire pit and several floors, but none of that matters as long as there is a dance floor and music. I push through to where it is the thickest, where it is the loudest, where you can feel the music in your teeth, where it overpowers your heartbeat, where it takes over. I don't want my own heartbeat tonight. I want it to pulse and pump outside of me.

Everything is spinning out of control. First Adam (I wonder where he is—no, I don't, don't think about Adam, it's not safe to think about him). Then Annie. I can't keep the threads I'm supposed to follow together, I can't pull them and yank them to what I want them to be, I can't follow what I'm supposed to do.

I have no idea.

I used to be so good at knowing exactly how to do what was best for Annie and me, but I have no idea who *me* is anymore, and Annie, why would she want me to kill him? If I don't know who we are, how can I know our track?

I start moving. Swaying. Finding the music, losing myself.

"DRINK?"

I turn, surprised to see my line boy still behind me. He stopped existing for me as soon as I got what I wanted. "I don't—" I don't drink. Annie made me promise not to, and I haven't, not a drop, not a single drop since that first time. Not even the year we were apart. Annie also promised to take care of me. Then she sent me out to kill someone.

"ABSOLUTELY!" I shout. He smiles and he thinks it's predatory, and if I were another girl, I would-should-could be worried. I am the predator in any situation. I am not worried.

I close my eyes and sway, let the music wash out everything else, let it give me the dull I look for everywhere, let it pound the very thoughts from my brain. My only job right now, the only thing I have to do, is move.

So I move.

I move slow. I move fast. I move faster. My shoulder burns and I can't raise that arm much, but I don't care, can't care. I am rhythm and bass and drums and beats and I don't care what the song is, I just move.

Something breaks through, breaks me out, and I'm livid. I turn to find the boy from the line. He's shouting something. I don't care what he has to say. He leans closer and shouts again.

"YOU'RE CRAZY SEXY OUT HERE."

I raise an eyebrow. "One part of that description is correct."

"WHAT?"

He's holding two glasses. I grab one. The way he watches it, I know he put something extra in it. All the better. I tip my head back and bring the glass up and—

"STOP." Someone grabs my arm, the drink splashes me. It smells sharp and sour and sweet all at the same time, and now there's that much less of it to drink. I scowl up to see James.

"He put something in it," James yells.

I roll my eyes. "Of course he did." I turn to the line boy, but, oh dear, he's on the ground, clutching a bleeding nose. I shake my head and tsk at James. "That's no way to make friends!"

"We're leaving."

He still has my arm, my uninjured one, and he's pulling me toward the door. I spin away from his grasp and back into the bodies, turning and beckoning him with a grin. He shakes his head.

I raise both arms in the air (it hurts but I don't care), bring them up through my hair, let my hips catch the beat. Look at James through my eyelashes. I have never let James dance with me before, not once, but I might die tomorrow and Annie used me and I can never be with someone like Adam, so I don't care tonight.

He bites his lip. He follows me.

He puts his hands on my hips and I keep my arms in the air and there is the beat, the beat, the beat, and the music. And there is his body next to mine, and it isn't just a body, it's *his* body.

I wanted this so many times. Too many times. I never let myself have it. After a song or three or seven, James pulls me closer. "We should get you home."

"You should buy me a drink!"

"You aren't supposed to drink."

"Thanks, Annie! I'm also not supposed to do this." I put my hands on his chest (my hands he knows all about and he doesn't push me away), and stretch up, take his earlobe between my teeth.

"Fia," he says, and I don't know if he's scolding me or moaning.

"Buy me a drink." I bite his ear harder. I feel like I'm in control tonight. I feel like *I* am the one using *him* tonight. I feel good. Or as good as I ever do.

He leans his face into mine—his cheek has a hint of stubble, it's rough, I want to run my mouth along it—then bends down, lets his lips touch my neck, trace it ever so lightly.

He grabs my hand and pulls me out of the crowd, toward the bar. He's angry, with himself or with me I can't tell, but I'm getting my way so I don't care. "Since we're breaking all the rules anyway."

"That's the spirit!"

"Annie will kill me."

"No, she'll just have me do it."

He squints suspiciously at me, but I smile and twirl away to get to the drinks faster.

"Only one," he says.

I open my blue eyes wide. I am the picture of innocent earnestness. "Absolutely."

I can't dance anymore. The lights are spinning and the floor is spinning. How did they install a spinning floor? It's amazing. The whole world spins, spins, spins from the balcony where we're sitting. I try to tap, but I can't find my leg with my finger, and I laugh. I'm even free from my three taps.

"You know why I don't want to be with you?" James's eyes are as glassy as they were the first time we met.

"Because I'm too young for you? Because you're an evil, manipulative monster and I know it?"

He smiles, and his smile has that edge I know, that sharp edge I recognize. It sings to my own sharp soul. "You knowing makes me want you more. And you aren't young. You haven't been young since you were fourteen."

I smile back. "Fine, then. Because I'm psychotic and I kill people?"

"Nope." He shakes his head, still smiling. "Because my dad wants us together."

"Seriously?"

"Yeah. He suggested it when we left on the yacht. Wanted you to fall in love with me as another way to tie you to us."

I laugh. "Wasn't he worried I'd kill you in your sleep or something?"

"I don't think he'd actually care."

"Oh, poor James." I scoot across the dark velvet of the love seat, scoot right onto James's lap, wrap my arms around his neck. "Why do you care if he cares? Your dad is *evil*." Is it the money? Can he not live without bottomless funds? Or does he actually believe in this shadowy network of power his dad is building? I need to know. I let myself ignore it for so long, but the why is killing me. The why of James working for his father. The why of how I can feel like this for him even though he is part of what did this to me.

He looks at my lips, leans in closer. I don't need to know the why anymore. I don't care. I'll care again tomorrow, but now? I close my eyes, waiting, waiting, wanting his lips on mine.

He pecks my nose instead, then laughs. I open my eyes and glare.

"My dad *is* evil. But I'm a Keane. It's my duty to care. I owe it to my mother."

"So, are you finally living up to Daddy Dearest's dearest wishes? Are you going to *seduce* me, James Keane?"

He pulls me in closer. "I've only stayed away from you this long because he wanted me to do the opposite. I can't let him win, can I?"

"I won't tell if you don't."

"But what about the Readers?"

"Oh, them? I think 'I'm boinking the boss's son!' at them every chance I get. But only the ones who are in love with you."

"You are evil." But he looks at me like I'm not.

I know it's wrong.

He's a Keane.

He isn't his father, but he will be.

He's almost as good a liar as I am, and I am too drunk to sift through what he's said.

It's wrong, wrong, wrong.

But his hands are on my neck and in my hair and tracing my collarbone and it is wrong but it feels right, it feels like falling and I know the impact at the bottom will probably kill me, but I don't care anymore.

"I've wanted to kiss you since that first night in the school. I've wanted to kiss you every single day since then." He shifts me even closer. We are touching, touching everywhere and it's wrong it's wrong it's wrong but right right now and I close my eyes and his lips are even better at the dulling than the drinks or the music. His lips light me on fire and dull everything else and I lose myself in them, and I am so happy and relieved to be lost I could cry.

We stumble out onto the street, wrapped around each other, and I am light-headed and my feet can't trace a straight line, and I can't feel anything.

Right or wrong or even my hands.

It's glorious.

I laugh.

James nuzzles his face into the top of my head, breathing in my hair. "You're amazing, you know that? I think I love you."

I push him into the wall, grab his shirt in my fists, kiss him hard. Pull away. He is such a liar. "You don't love me, you idiot. No one does. No one should."

"That's not true. I do love you. I'm just trying so hard not to. It would ruin everything. But you don't make it easy, you know?"

I laugh and walk a few steps ahead. This late/early there is no one out but a car on the corner. Delivery van.

Idling.

It's wrong, it shouldn't be there, I know it shouldn't. No one would deliver something right now on these streets. I turn to James. "Something's wrong." I know it in my stomach sloshing with drinks.

"Nothing's wrong." He reaches out to pull me into his arms and I jump forward and put my foot behind his, trip him as I shove him down.

Someone swings a fist where his head was.

I lift my foot and kick backward as hard as I can with my sharp heel (the sharp heels—I needed the sharp heels), and it slams into something and then there's a wet give as it breaks through skin and someone shouts but it's muffled. I yank my foot back and the shoe doesn't come with it. I kick the other one off because now it will only slow me down.

Am I screaming? I should be screaming. James is shouting, trying to get up. The man who swung at James's head pulls something out of his jacket and points it at James and I can't lose James, I won't, not now that I found his lips. I throw myself onto the man, wrap my arms and legs around him. He's off balance and stumbling, and I sink my teeth into his shoulder as hard as I can.

I shouldn't have had anything to drink. Annie was right. This is not a fight I should lose.

He slams me into the brick wall and the air leaves my lungs in a sad, drunken whoosh. I drop off and hit the ground on crouched legs. I need to protect James. I need to get them away from James.

I run (I can still run, I know how to run, I can do this) toward the opposite side of the street, away from the van. Glance back, they've left James, he's up now and stumbling toward us, but he had even more to drink than I did and they are not drunk, they are definitely not drunk.

I can get away. I know I can. One of them has stopped, turned to face James. Does he have a gun? He might have a gun. I don't know, I can't tell.

If I run now, I'll only be followed by one and I can take him down and get away.

I turn and spin past the man following me, dive for the knees of the man facing James. He falls; I am tangled up in him.

"RUN!" I scream at James. "I'm behind you!"

He waits until I'm up and then he runs and I am behind him.

And someone is behind me, arms circling my waist, lifting me off the ground. Cloth-covered hand over my mouth, pulling me backward. I am swimming and it smells stinging sweet and someone else has my legs. I can't remember how to kick, it's getting too dark. A light, a slamming door. James, where is James? I can't breathe I can't keep my eyes open.

The last thing I see is the girl with brown eyes and brown hair whose car I stole.

FIA

Two Years Ago

~

WHY DOES HATING THE MOST VIOLENT THING I'VE ever done make me want to be violent?

They took away my computer when they realized I was researching jail time for various crimes. But they didn't have to. I have nowhere to go. Annie is here.

Annie told me to get out of her life.

If I really thought she'd be safe here, if I really thought she'd be okay on her own?

I don't know.

My closet is dark and warm. I like sitting in it. Sometimes I sleep here. Sleep, sleep. I'll sleep now.

"Fia?"

I startle, smack my head against the wall. Ouch.

"Annie?" I push open the closet door. She's standing in the middle of my room. She has one hand out, palm up, the way she always comes into a room where she knows I am. She's waiting for my hand.

I hide my horrible hands behind my back. "What?"

She looks scared. Nervous. I stand and rush out of the closet. "What's wrong? What did you see?"

"I—I didn't see anything. I heard. Fia, what have they been doing to you? What have they made you do? Tell me. Please tell me." Her voice cracks and if she cries, I will cry and I won't, I won't let myself cry.

"Bad things," I whisper. "I'll never tell you."

She holds out both her hands and I trip forward, let her wrap her arms around me. "Okay. Okay. You don't have to tell me. It doesn't matter. We're leaving. Today."

"Really? You want to leave?" My heart expands, bursts— hope, there is hope, I have hope for the first time in years. We're going to leave! Annie wants to leave, so it won't be betraying her, won't be taking her away from hope for her eyes.

"Pack your things," she says. "I've got all my stuff ready. We can probably sell my laptop and braille equipment for a few thousand dollars. Enough to get back to Aunt Ellen's. Once we're there, we'll figure out how to get ahold of her. I'll leave a note for Eden so she knows why we left and can find us if she wants to leave, too."

My heart sinks. "You packed? When did you decide we should run?"

"Last night. I've been up all night, reading train and bus schedules. Do you have any cash at all? There's a Greyhound station. It's a long walk, but we can do it. And you can figure out how to sell my laptop, right?"

She sounds so hopeful, so determined. I back away and slump on my unmade bed. "We can't. They already know."

Annie frowns, shakes her head. "No, we need to leave. We need to get you out of here."

"We should have run last night, the moment you thought of it. It's too late now. They already know what we'll do. Clarice will be watching. So we can't do it."

"But—"

"No. Not today."

Annie's shoulders collapse. She tries to walk over to my bed but trips on a pile of shoes. I haven't been keeping the floor clean. It's dangerous for her. Bad, bad Fia.

"Sorry. Here." I take her hand, lead her to the bed. She sits next to me, every line of her body turned down.

"I've ruined everything. I'm so sorry."

"Hey." I put my arm around her shoulders. It's my job to take care of her. And I will. "It's okay. Now that I know you don't want to be here, I can fix this." I smile; she can't see how wicked my smile is. "I'll get us out of here. You need to be ready to go at a second's notice. It won't be easy. I don't think we can go back home." She has to understand. I know—I can feel—they'll never just let me go. We'll have to hide.

Forever.

But if we hide together, then it's not hiding. It's escaping.

She nods, sits up straighter. "Anytime. I'm ready. And, Fia?"

I am trying not to think of escaping. I am not planning anything. I am letting the future be a complete blank. If I have no plans, they cannot see my plans. I live now and only now. "What?"

"I know we have a future. And whatever you've done, whatever you think you're guilty of? You're not. It's not your fault. You know that, right? You're a good person."

My eyes sting and my throat aches and my heart hurts and she is wrong but I want her to be right. I want it so badly, it *has* to become true. When we leave here, we will leave all this, and things won't be wrong all the time, buzzing constantly at the back of my mind and in my hands and in my stomach with the wrongness of everything. I will feel right. I will be good.

As I finish randomly picking stocks, Clarice smiles at me like she knows something I don't. I know what she thinks she knows that I don't. I know she saw us leave, that she's expecting it at any time.

I smile back at her. I hope that she's personally taking the extra patrol duties or whatever security measures they've put in place. Because it's a waste of time. I can be patient. Annie is on my side now. I can wait and wait and not plan a thing. I am not planning a thing.

"You seem cheerful this morning," she says, taking another sip of her coffee.

"If you were a Reader, you'd know it was because I put something in your drink."

She glances in horror at her half-empty cup before her face smooths itself out and she smiles again. "I like your sense of humor."

"Are we done? Because my nap isn't going to take itself." I stretch in my chair, put my legs up on her desk, my skirt riding up my thighs but I don't care, because I am finally back in control.

"You keep thinking that word," Ms. Robertson says from behind me and I freeze. I hadn't heard the door open. Clarice must not have closed it all the way. "Control. What an interesting word for you to be dwelling on."

"I have some other words." I scream the F-word in my head, over and over and over again.

"We have an assignment for you," Clarice says, but I am too busy screaming thoughts to pay much attention. "There's a girl. We need her."

I start at the beginning, mentally screaming every obscenity

I can in alphabetical order. Then I start setting them to the tune of "Row, Row, Row Your Boat."

"Are you listening, Sofia?"

I nod.

"This girl we need, her family has declined our generous scholarship. So we've been forced to go to extreme measures to help her. You're going to kidnap her."

I laugh, abruptly cutting off the chorus of my song. "I am, am I?"

"Yes. We've got all the information here. Pictures, important details about Sadie and her family. I'll leave it to your discretion how to go about it all, but I will note that it might be easier for everyone involved if there were some sort of accident that meant she had no more family to ask questions or look for her."

Some sort of accident.

Some sort of accident.

Some sort of accident.

My brain sticks on that phrase, like a skipping CD, repeating it over and over.

"We didn't know about you and your sister then," Ms. Robertson says from behind me. "In your case it was your parents' accident and the news story about the blind girl who saw it that caught our attention."

I laugh. It's high and fast and strange. "Well, then, that's all right. I'll set a gas fire, maybe? Blow them all up! Then it would be efficient *and* pretty. And the girl—Sadie?—we can roast marshmallows before skipping back here and introducing her to her new home!"

"Sofia," Clarice says, and her voice is low with warning.

"Clarice," I answer, and my voice is not low with warning—my voice is high with giddy hysteria, but my eyes are knives. "I'm not doing it."

"That's not an option."

I stand up, kick my chair over. It skitters across the floor and crashes into the wall. She jumps, stands, and backs away. I like that she's scared of me.

"I'm going back to my room now. I'll keep playing your stupid stocks games or your sick little physical challenges because I don't have anywhere else to go. But if you think for one second I am *ever* hurting someone for you again, you're wrong. I won't do it. *And you can't make me.*"

I turn and walk past Ms. Robertson, thinking CONTROL as loudly as I can at her.

"We'll see," Clarice says, her soft voice carrying through to the hall. "Remember. It's your choice that did this. You did this."

She's crazy. Crazy crazy. And I don't care. I skip down the wide, empty hallway, singing at the top of my lungs. I know I'm not free yet, but I feel like I am. This feeling, this huge horrible wrong nagging feeling I've had since I was twelve will go away and I'll be able to breathe, I'll be able to think, I'll be able to use whatever it is they think I have for myself. I'll use it to make my own path. I'll never do it for anyone else, not ever again.

But the wrong feeling is getting wronger. I feel like the ground has been pulled out from underneath me. My heart races. I can't breathe. Something is wrong.

It's wrong wrong wrong WRONG WRONG WRONG! I need to find Annie.

I race up the stairs, through the hall, burst through her door. She's there. Annie's there, in her room, she's okay, what's wrong?

She's sitting on her bed. Her face is blank.

"Are you okay? Annie?"

"I saw myself." Her voice is as blank as her face.

"You—what?"

"I saw myself. In a vision. At first I thought it was you, but the hair was too short." She lifts a hand to her hair that hits at her shoulders. "And the eyes were different. But it looked so much like you. Then I realized. It was me. I finally saw what I look like."

I sit down, still dizzy with panic. "Told you you're beautiful." What is wrong? Nothing is wrong here. Why isn't my body calming down?

She doesn't react. "I was dead."

I can't breathe. I can't breathe, I can't breathe. "What?"

"I was dead. There was a hole in my head. A perfect red hole. And my hair, it's darker than I thought it was, it was all tangled up in the blood on the floor. There wasn't as much blood as you'd think there would be. I was dead. They killed me." She closes her eyes. "I'm going to die."

"How would that happen? How would that even—"

I said no.

I told them no.

I thought I was in control.

They are always in control.

"What else? Any other details? Any other details at all? Do you know when it happens? Where? Anything!" She doesn't react, so I grab her shoulders, shake her. "TELL ME ANY-THING. GIVE ME SOMETHING."

"How can I tell you where it happens? I've never seen the room before. I've never seen *any* rooms before." She laughs drily. "The only other detail was Clarice. She was standing next to my body, talking to someone on the phone."

"Did she shoot you?"

"I don't know."

My heart picks up. Races. Don't plan. Don't plan. "But she was there? In the room?"

"Yes."

I run out. Back down the stairs. I don't think. I don't plan. I just run. Back to the classroom. Clarice is still there. She looks up at me, a single eyebrow raised. "Have you changed your mind then?"

I pick up the chair on the ground, still against the wall where I kicked it. I lift it and spin and smash it into Clarice's head.

She doesn't even have time to look surprised.

I smash it on her again and again and again.

And then I stop and drop the chair and sink to the floor. Clarice's lifeless eyes stare at me from her bloodied and ruined head.

If Clarice is dead, she can't be there when Annie gets shot. That can't happen now.

It won't happen now.

Annie is safe.

Annie is safe. Annie is safe. Annie is safe. Annie is safe. Annie is safe. Annie is safe. Annie is safe. Annie is safe. Annie is safe. Annie is safe. Annie is safe. Annie is safe.

ANNIE
Monday Evening

~

I KNOW ALL MY INTERNET ACTIVITY IS MONITORED and that I can't search anything on Adam without raising suspicion. I wish Fia and I had been able to talk. She could have told me more about him, maybe told me *why* he was connected to all those women who didn't want to be found. She said he was nice.

He looked nice.

I can't search for him. But I search for Lerner. Keane can't get angry: he's the one who gave me the name.

I search Lerner + psychics.

Lerner + mind readers.

Lerner + psychic phenomenon.

Lerner + paranormal abilities.

Lerner + every single word I can think of that might give me any insight whatsoever into who they are and why they are interested in Adam. I don't know if he's with them now, but he *will* be. And they know my sister's name.

I read and search until my finger is numb. Nothing. There is nothing. Fia would know what to do. She'd figure out how to get the information she needed to keep me safe. I, on the other hand, am sitting alone in my room in the building I cannot leave, doing internet searches on psychics.

My parents were right. Fia is special. I can't take care of anyone.

"Where is she?" Hands grab me, pull me up off the couch. I try to hit them away. I don't know what's going on, who is here, where I am.

Asleep. On the couch. I fell asleep waiting for Fia to call me back so I could somehow tell her about Adam.

"James?"

"Fia's gone. You need to find her. *Now.*"

My mind spins, clunking past the remains of sleep. I feel slow. "I saw her dancing. Did you check clubs?"

"She *was* dancing. With me. And then we were attacked on the street and they threw her in a van and drove away."

"Are you drunk? Were you both drunk?" I push him out of my way and stand, whip my hand out until I find his face. Hit him. "YOU LET HER GET DRUNK?"

"Why aren't you looking for her yet? FIND HER!"

"It doesn't work like that! I told her not to go dancing! This is your fault. You let her go out. You got her drunk. If she hadn't been drinking, there's no way they could have taken her." I slap him again. "This is your fault."

He grabs my wrist and his hand squeezes too hard; he's going to hit me back. Then he sinks onto the couch. "Please." His voice is tortured. "It is. It's my fault. She could have gotten away but she came back to protect me. She shouldn't have come back."

"You're right. She shouldn't have. You're not worth it."

He doesn't answer. I want to hit him again, to scream. He lost Fia. He lost her. Then, finally, he says, "Is there anything you know—anything you saw? We have to get her back."

Being watched while dancing. And . . . Adam. The vision with Adam. They were asking about Fia. That's the connection. It has to be. But I can't tell James that Adam is alive without telling him that Fia lied about killing him. And if they know that Fia lied and didn't do what they asked . . .

The only image I have of my own face floats in my memory, cold and terrible. But just as terrible is knowing what Fia did to keep that from happening. I can't let them push her that far again.

"Do you care about my sister?"

"Of course I do," he snaps. I wish I could see his face. I wish I could read people like Fia does, know when they are lying. She says James is always lying. But she likes that about him.

"Did you kiss her?" I ask, whispering.

A pause. "Yes."

"Do you remember how old she is? She's a *kid*, James. A seriously screwed up kid."

His voice is thicker. Maybe with guilt. I don't know. I've never been able to get much other than false flirting and anger from his voice. "Yes."

"Do you remember how she was when you first came back here?"

"Yes, yes, *yes*! Can you find her or not?"

"She didn't kill Adam Denting."

"She—what?"

"She didn't kill him. She said she got there and she couldn't. That's why she's so off, so crazy. Not because she killed him. Because she thinks she killed me again by not doing what your father wants her to."

There's a long pause. "Why did my father take the hit out? Maybe I can fix it."

"I told him Adam would destroy him."

"He's going to—wait. You *told* my father that. Was it true?"

"No."

He swears, and I flinch and cover my head as my lamp

smashes against the wall. "You tricked him into sending Fia out on a hit? What is wrong with you? Do you know how long I've worked to get her this stable, and you send her out to kill someone? Why? What on earth could possibly justify risking your sister? *I* should be asking *you* if you care about her."

"I didn't think they'd send her!" I shout. "Why would they send *her*? Why would they risk her like that?"

"What did you think would happen when you told my father that someone was going to destroy him? Of course he'd risk her. You're really something, Annie. All these years Fia thought she was a killer. But she's only ever fought to protect you. And here you are, ordering hits."

"It wasn't like that," I whisper. "It was bigger than us. It *is* bigger than us. I wasn't doing it for me. Or even for Fia. I was doing it so Fia wouldn't happen to a thousand other girls."

"Your sister sacrificed everything for you. Glad to know you're looking out for a thousand strangers instead of her. Well done."

I swallow hard. "I saw Adam again. I don't know where he was. But I know who he was with. Does the name Lerner mean anything to you?"

He laughs. It's harsh and low and it sounds like Fia's and I ache and shatter and break on the inside. He's right. I've failed her in so many ways, too many ways to ever atone for.

I hear the couch creak as he stands. "Well, that's just brilliant.

Lerner has Fia. Do you want to tell my father, or should I?"

"You can't tell him about Adam. He'll kill me."

"I don't really care one way or the other what happens to you. But you dying would destroy Fia, so I'll do whatever I can to cover up your mess. Because *I care* about your sister."

I hang my head and cry. He leaves without a word.

I see Fia that night. I don't know if it's a dream or a vision, but she's alone, and she's scared, and she's crying.

But she isn't scared for herself.

She's scared that something will happen to *me* because she got kidnapped.

In the morning when I wake up again on the couch I immediately know I am not alone. I can smell tea, my favorite tea, and the tiny clink of a spoon stirring.

"Good morning, Annabelle."

Mr. Keane. Here. In my room. If I were going to die, would I have seen it? I can't die. I have to save Fia.

"James informed me of the unfortunate development with your sister. I'm very disappointed."

"Do you know where she is? Can you find her?" I sit up. I want to smooth my hair, to pull the blanket over myself so he can't see my bare arms, but I resist.

"I have everyone working on it. I'll be very upset if we lose

Sofia. And I expect you'll be pushing yourself to see something helpful."

"Of course."

"Very good. Because without Sofia, there really isn't a place for you here."

He doesn't say if there's not a place for me here, there's not a place for me anywhere. He doesn't have to. I swallow. I hope he doesn't see it.

I hear him stand, and almost sigh in relief because I know where he is now in relation to me, and it means he's leaving.

"There is another matter. The matter of Adam Denting."

James, James, how could you? "Yes?"

"I've heard some interesting things about him since he was killed. Did you know he was a neurologist? Studied brain abnormalities in women. Something of a prodigy. Very interesting. And I've been thinking about what you saw, his name swallowing mine. I'm curious: How can a girl who has been blind since age four understand a vision that revolves around words?"

I stutter, grasping desperately for something, anything to explain this. Fia would know. She'd have a lie. She'd twist and slide and slip through this. She'd never have messed up this bad in the first place.

I am lost.

His voice is close now, too close, and I sink back against the couch, wishing I could disappear into it. "If you ever try to manipulate me again, dear girl, I can assure you that your death will not be nearly so pleasant and fast as the last one you saw, and I will personally make certain it happens."

No footsteps, he has no footsteps, but I hear the door open with a click and a whisper. "If I were you, I'd pray for Sofia's swift return."

ANNIE
Eighteen Months Ago
~

I STOP HALFWAY TO FIA'S DOOR, THE TRAY BALANCED carefully on my hip. "You're new," I say. He smells like oranges and . . . something darker. Richer. Not the cheap, stinging aftershave of Stewart, the regular guard.

He laughs; it has an edge to it that sets my senses on alert. It's unnerving and a little bit sexy. I am eighteen years old. I know nothing about sexy. Or men. I wish I did. I wonder what it would be like to have a life where boys were a part of it.

This man, whoever he is, knows everything about sexy. I can already tell by his smell and his laugh. "I *am* new. How did you know I was here?"

"Stewart smells much worse. And he breathes like a horse."

He laughs again. "You must be Annabelle."

I smile, then inwardly berate myself. What am I doing? He's one of them. And, even worse, he's new. Which means something must be changing. Which is absolutely terrifying. "Why are you here?"

"They needed a replacement for the previous project manager."

The previous project manager. Clarice. Dead Clarice. "So, what did you do wrong to get assigned here?"

"Ah, you mean what did I do right? Because here is looking pretty good now."

I don't know if I'm blushing; my cheeks are hot and I feel like I need to tuck my hair behind my ear or touch my neck, but I'm holding the tray. Fia's tray. "I have to take this in to Fia. Open the door."

"Fia," he says experimentally, then repeats it softly to himself. "Yes, about that."

I feel the tray wobble ever so slightly. He touched it. "What did you just do?"

"I think it's time we weaned your sister off the sedatives, don't you?"

"Really?" I turn my face toward his voice, overwhelmed with hope. They've kept her so drugged up ever since . . . ever since that day. She's barely a person. I've asked and asked, pleaded, argued, demanded. What was the point in keeping her here if they were going to leave her a zombie forever?

"Really."

Tears spill down my face, warm tracks. I don't know what to do with myself. I bend and set the tray on the ground, then, on impulse, throw my arms in a hug around him. He is tall and solid, and being this close he smells even better. "Thank you."

"You're welcome, but I'm not doing it for you."

"Thank you, thank you, thank you." I let go and back away, suddenly embarrassed. "I'm sorry, I don't even know your name."

"James."

"The beautiful boy with the booze?" I ask, horrified. That's how Fia and I have referred to him ever since that night. And now he's in charge of our very lives.

I wish I could take back my hug.

"Come on. Please? No one describes movies as well as you do." I finish brushing Fia's hair, but she still sits listlessly on the end of the bed. I moved into a bigger dorm, more like an apartment, last month.

James let me move her out of the secure wing and back in with me five days ago. She hasn't seen him yet. I haven't told her he's in charge of us now. I still don't know what that means, how that changes things.

But thanks to him, she's off the sedatives. I just give her one at night to help her sleep. There's almost no difference between heavily sedated Fia and normal Fia, though.

"You act like nothing changed," she whispers.

"Why should I act like something changed?"

"You know what I did!"

I flinch away from her voice, but part of me is glad. At least I got a reaction. "It doesn't matter."

She laughs. It's low and empty and I wish she wouldn't ever laugh like that again. "You didn't do it."

"Let's move on. Forget about it. You're not going to be punished for it. Everyone understands. I talked with—I talked with Mr. Keane."

"*The* Mr. Keane?" she asks.

"Yes. On the phone, right after. I was so scared they'd—they'd take you away. I told him everything, about what you saw, about why you—why it happened. He wasn't angry!" Actually, he'd laughed, a silent whisper of a laugh. I couldn't get it out of my head. It was the only laugh I've ever heard worse than Fia's dead-girl laugh. "So we move on. Back to our plan. The plan not to have a plan. Remember?" I nudge her, smiling hopefully. She needs to have hope. She needs to have something.

Ever since it became obvious that I knew what this school really was and that I wasn't seeing anything other than the occasional glimpse of Fia, they've pretty much ignored me. I can do whatever I want as long as I stay in a few select (and guarded) wings of the building. But they don't pretend to care about my future anymore—no new tech, no more visits from the doctor. I wonder if there ever was any hope for my eyes. Probably just another lie woven to keep me invested and Fia trapped.

Just another future I've lost.

"You can't see my hands," Fia whispers. There's a noise, almost too quiet to hear. A tiny tap-tap-tap, like she's playing a beat on her leg.

I try to reach out for her fingers, but she snatches them away.

"You can't see my hands, and you didn't see her face. Remember that night we fought? Just before? You said you'd be okay without me. Did you mean it?"

"Fia, sweetheart, let's don't talk about that. That was a long time ago."

She sighs. "I want to sleep now."

I leave her alone. I'll figure it out. I try to research post-traumatic stress disorder online, but nothing fits. I don't know how to help her. Nothing I'm doing is working.

And the thing is, I can't ever tell her, but she didn't *need* to do what she did. Just knowing that they'd kill me if she didn't do what they wanted her to would have changed things. Killing Clarice wasn't the only option. If she had asked me, if she had just waited and talked about it, I'm sure I would have told her not to do it.

I think she knows. She picked the first way to stop that vision from ever happening. But she didn't pick the only way.

The other way would have been doing whatever it was they wanted her to. I hope it was worse than what she did. I really do. Because the option she chose is destroying her.

That night when I go to get her sleeping pill, the brand-new bottle is empty.

"Please," I say. "Get off the couch. We haven't been outside since you were sick." *Since you ate a bottle of sleeping pills. Since you tried to leave me in the only way you could.* "Let's go walk the grounds." The school is a square with an open courtyard in the middle. They let us go out there. Maybe if I can get her in the sunshine, maybe if we can feel it and she can see it, maybe it will help.

"Eden can take you."

"I don't want to go with Eden."

She doesn't even answer. I don't know what to do anymore. This is worse than when she was sedated, worse than anything, because there's nothing to fight, nothing to rally against. She's completely lost herself, and I don't know how to bring her back.

Someone knocks and I shout for them to come in, hoping it's Eden and I can get a break from this frustrating, mind-numbingly awful existence. But the clomp-clomp-clomp of heavy, confident steps and the scent of oranges and velvet night air flood my apartment.

"James?" Fia's voice is incredulous.

"Apparently I am to be addressed as the Beautiful Boy with the Booze. But I take it Annabelle didn't tell you I was back."

Of course I didn't tell her. I've heard all the girls talking about him. He flirts shamelessly with everyone. The Readers whisper that he thinks constantly about sex. Eden says he reeks of lust. I don't want him in my rooms. I don't want him around my baby sister.

"Unfortunately," he says, "this time I didn't find any bottles of whiskey to steal before visiting. Can I still come in?"

An exhalation. Was that a laugh? Not the hollow dead-girl laugh?

"I don't care," she says.

"Excellent." I hear the couch's leather creak. How close is he sitting to her? Is he touching her? I want him away from her. I wish I had been sitting on the couch next to her so I could block him, shield her from him.

"To what do we owe the honor?" I ask.

"I was bored. Running this school is dead dull."

Fia's voice is sharper than it's been in weeks. "Since when do you work for your father?"

"Didn't you hear? I own the school. Twenty-one now, and I've come into my mother's idea of an inheritance. I would've preferred my own island, but there are perks to this." There is a pause here; no one says anything; and I have never felt so blind as I do now, trying to imagine how he is looking at her when he says "perks."

Finally James talks again. "Now, Fia. I've got a confession." I stiffen, furious. He can't call her that. He doesn't deserve to use her nickname.

"Hmm?"

"The first night we met, when I told you my name, do you remember what you said?"

She doesn't answer.

"You said, 'I should bash your brains in right now.' I apologize for assuming you were a liar and a flirt. I see now you were quite serious, and I must have offended you dearly."

My jaw drops in horror. How could he? How could he joke about that? After what she did?

"I hereby vow to take any and all death threats at face value, unless you are, in fact, trying to flirt with me, in which case please threaten to bash my brains in while winking, like so."

And then—

She laughs. She actually laughs, not like she did before we came here but like she did before things got really bad. It's harder and has jagged edges, but it's a laugh.

"I've gotta tell you, when I heard what happened, I thought my father would be more upset, but do you know what he said to me? 'She should have seen it coming.'"

"That's terrible!" I hiss.

Fia laughs louder. "*Someone* taught me how to get in trouble around a Seer."

"And you are a star pupil. You surpassed even my record, which I used to be quite proud of. If we're still keeping score, this puts you firmly in the lead and I owe you this drink."

I slash my hand through the air. "Stop." Did he bring alcohol in here? That joke about the whiskey—is he making fun of me because I can't see that he's holding some? "You will *not* give her anything."

"Relax. I've come with ice-cold Coke. Not even as a mixer. Just as a drink."

"While we're talking about that night," Fia says, and her voice doesn't sound like it's coming from miles away. It sounds like she's here, now, in this room. "I seem to recall you saying you'd like to kiss me but you needed to get through a couple more drinks before you could let yourself. Have you had enough time to down them?"

James laughs; their laughs are a matching set. It makes me feel small and alone. Jealous. I'm jealous of James Keane. Why can he make her laugh like a real person? I've been taking care of her all this time and I was barely keeping her alive. He's one of *them*!

"I think," he says, "if I kept up my end of that promise, Annie here would take your place in bashing my brains out."

"I already called dibs on it. She would never dare." She's

teasing him. She sounds like the old Fia. He swoops in here, talking about bashing in heads and drinking, and draws her out? Why would she come out for him but not for her own sister?

"Excellent. I'd hate for anyone else to have the honor. Now. Since I've got you here, I have a proposal."

"Too young to get married. Besides, Annie loathes you and everyone else would be too frightened to be my maid of honor. I have a bit of a *reputation*." She whispers "reputation" exaggeratedly. How can she flirt with him about this?

"Oh, that *is* a problem. In that case, I have a different proposal. How would you like to go on a vacation? Sort of a study abroad. I think you've been locked up in this school for too long. It isn't healthy, you know. Some would say it'll drive you crazy."

"When?" she asks, and her voice is breathless and hopeful. I'm drowning. I'm losing her, and I don't know how or why.

"How soon can you pack?"

She jumps up with a squeal and I hear her run out of the room. "Just the basics," James yells. "We can buy anything you need."

"What are you doing?" I hiss.

"What you can't." I hear him stand. He walks closer to me, puts a hand on my shoulder. "I'm going to make her better."

I shrug his hand off, glare up at his voice. "How? By making sick jokes about things no one should ever have to remember?

And why do you want her 'better'? So you can use her again? You saw how well that turned out for the last person in charge here."

"Careful there, Annabelle. You can't *pretend* to not care about what Fia did. You've either got to really not care at all, or you've got to care. She knows you're somewhere in between, and her own guilt is already more than she can handle."

"Don't act like you know her! She's my sister!"

"In case you haven't noticed, you lost your claim to her as soon as you accepted the Keane Foundation's generosity. She's not yours. After your desperate call to my father, he decided to give me a bigger role in his work. She's my responsibility now. Don't worry. I take my responsibilities very seriously."

It can't be my fault that he's here. That's not what I wanted when I talked to his horrible father. "I won't let you have her."

"You don't have any choice." He sounds almost sorry when he says this. He is a liar.

"If you touch her—if you so much as touch her—" I am trembling with rage. "Don't you dare. Don't you dare ever forget how young she is or how broken she is."

His voice isn't sorry anymore. "How could I? And how could she, with such a kind sister to remind her that she is hopelessly broken."

"I'm ready!" Her voice is bright. I hear something thunk to the ground. Her bag.

I whip around. "Don't go! You can't go!"

"Aren't you coming?" she asks.

"I'm sorry," James says, and he walks away from me. Is he touching her? Is he touching her? "But my father would only agree to let me take you if Annie stayed here and kept up her studies. And she needs to be here in case they have a breakthrough for her eye treatments."

"Oh." There's a pause, and then her voice . . . oh, her voice is dead again, it's coming from somewhere so deep inside and far away I can barely tell it's hers. "I guess I'll stay then."

"No." I choke on the word, paste a smile on my face, glad I can't see what she looks like, wishing she couldn't see me, either. She'll know I'm lying. She always knows when I'm lying. So she knows I'm lying every time I tell her that what she did doesn't matter, that we're going to be okay, that we're going to get out of here eventually. Please, Fia, believe this lie. "You should go. You've earned a vacation. Just bring me back a present. Besides, I'll have Eden."

"Afraid not," James says. "She's coming, too."

Alone. He's stealing my sister and my only friend. I'm going to be here all alone. I force my smile even bigger. "Well, then they'll both owe me a present."

"Are you sure?" Fia asks.

I am not sure. I don't trust James. I think he's even more dangerous than his father because he is bright and handsome and funny. I'm trying to draw her out with love and hope, but this place kills those. His voice has those extra layers, that anger simmering under the surface. I know Fia connects to it. I know it draws her in and comforts her in a way I never can. If I let her walk out that door with him, I'm worried I'll never get her back.

But James was right. I lost her the minute I brought her here with me. And if he can salvage something of who she used to be, no matter what his game is, I have to let him. I won't waste this time. I'm going to figure out what, exactly, is going on here. Because if I understand the what, I can understand the why, and if I understand those I can figure out the way to get us both free to a better future.

"Have fun. I love you. Don't forget your promises." I jerk my head in James's direction. No kissing. No drinking. She'll remember. "And don't plan anything without me."

She runs and hugs me—she hasn't hugged me in so long, and she is too thin, and taller, and I don't recognize her body anymore but maybe, just maybe, her voice will come back—and then she is gone and I am alone.

FIA
Tuesday Morning
~

JAMES. (MY HEAD, MY HEAD, IT HURTS SO MUCH.)

James.

Where is James?

Where am I?

I open my eyelids; they are sticky and they don't want to open and they hurt and the light—

Stabs of pain. Nausea roils through me. I don't want to feel like this, I can't feel like this, I can't remember why I feel like this. If I feel like this, I can't tell if something is wrong.

James. *Oh, no.* James.

I force my eyes open. I'm in a room. Alone. No windows (no escape points, no glass to use as a weapon), no furniture (maybe they have heard of my reputation with furniture), just smooth white walls and hard, dark-gray industrial carpet. And a door.

I stand. My head swims and the room tilts and swirls around me, and Annie was right, she is always right—I should not have gone dancing, I should not have gotten drunk, I should not have kissed James.

James said he loves me. He was probably lying.

I do not regret kissing James.

If they have hurt James, I will kill them.

Kill them kill them—wait. Annie. If I'm gone, Annie's not safe. What if James is with me? What if he can't tell them that I was taken, that I didn't run? Oh, no, Annie. Annie!

The door is locked. I scream and smash my hand against the handle, then slam my shoulder into it. I careen off, the room still spinning, but I have to get out. I can't lose Annie because I wanted to dance and kiss James. How could I have been so stupid and selfish? Everything was already screwed up; we were already in trouble. I can't believe I did this. I did this. Again. How many times will Annie have to see her own death because of me?

And Adam. I picture him checking his email, frantically, never hearing from me. He'll give up on me. He'll go back to his old life, and they'll find him, and they'll kill him. I've failed Annie and I've failed Adam. I destroy anything that's good.

Door opens inward. Can't break through. If I kick the

doorknob off (no shoes, I will break a few bones in my foot), they'll have to take down the door to get in. Lots of advance warning, and they can't keep the door shut again.

The hinges. I drop down and look at the bottom one. Simple straight metal pin down the center. I tug. It's painted shut. I can probably break the seal with my fingernails, but it'll take a while. I wish I had a tool. Something. Anything.

My fingers go to my hair, to the tiny bobby pin I tucked in last night to keep a twist of hair back from my face. I smile. I knew that was a good idea.

The top hinge pin will be a problem; I have nothing to stand on to reach that high. If I can get the bottom one out, I'll have options, though.

Break the doorknob, pull on the door to warp it, maybe make enough room to crawl out? It would take a lot time. If they're watching, they will know before I finish.

Stop! Stop planning. Just get the pin.

My fingers hurt and my head pounds and Annie, oh, Annie, I'm so sorry. How many ways can I fail you in one lifetime before it's too many, before I can't fix it? I sit back, lean my head against the wall, let myself cry. The weight of Annie's life pushes my shoulders down, wraps itself around me, sneaks into my heart and my lungs until I am suffocating.

I wipe under my eyes, wipe above them, try to get as much of the makeup off as I can. Try to look like a seventeen-year-old girl who is scared and alone and helpless.

Only one of those is a lie.

I get the pin out just as I hear the click of the lock on the other side of the door, then the slide of a dead bolt (dead bolt, glad I didn't try to kick in the doorknob). Rush or play dead? Rush or play dead?

I hide the hinge pin in my fist and scramble backward into the corner. They'll be most ready, most wary when they open the door. I'll have another chance. I curl into a ball, hug my bare legs to my chest. I'm glad I was crying, it will add to the look.

I stare up with my big, innocent eyes (they don't know about my hands; my eyes are my best liars). The door opens.

It's the girl, the one with brown hair whose car I stole. And behind her the man with the stubble. Cole. So much for feigning helplessness. I stand, keeping my hands fisted. They both walk into the room; neither has weapons. That was smart of them. Too bad. Cole has a slight limp (I wonder where my knife went; I liked that knife).

"Hello, Sofia." The girl has a soft voice. It's kind and cautious, but she's still looking at me in a strange way, not the way she should. She should be scared or angry. She has—what? A sense of wonder? Compassion? And still that recognition.

"I need to go to the bathroom," I say. "I kind of had a lot to drink last night." I take a step forward, let myself wobble as much as I should.

"Please stay where you are." Cole's voice is no-nonsense, and he . . . Hmmm. I don't feel any threat coming off him, not like before. He's not dangerous to me right now. Interesting. In fact, the only thing I'm worried about right now is Annie.

"Okay." I lean back against the wall, narrow my eyes at both of them. "I don't have very much time. Why am I here? Where is James?"

"We left James on the street." Cole sees the shift in my expression and quickly adds, "Alive."

So they weren't after James. It was about me.

"We found you because of James," the woman says. "We linked him to the school and have been tracking him for a while. So when I saw him at the club and recognized you, we finally had the break we needed." She pauses, frowns. "You're very hard to see."

Well, that's wonderful. She's a Seer. I should have known. "It's a talent."

"What are you? We know you're with Keane's school. And that you don't want to be. We know about your sister—"

"You know nothing about my sister," I snarl.

She continues on, softer. "We know that you were both taken five years ago. But in your case we don't know why. I've seen you. A few times. Just flashes, just enough to know you're important without knowing why. What do you do?"

"You mean am I a Seer or a Reader or a Feeler? They'd be the eyes, ears, and soul of an operation? I guess you could say I'm the hands."

I spring forward, grab the woman, spin her around between Cole and me, the pin out of my hand and pressed against her neck. (Can't tap tap tap my hand—I don't want to add another tap but I will; if it saves Annie, I will.) "It's not sharp but I can push it in, all the way. She'll bleed to death."

"It's okay," she says. She sounds remarkably calm. I kind of like her, actually. Cole raises his hands and backs a step away.

I angle us toward the door, keeping her body between Cole and me, always between us. "I don't want to hurt you. But my sister needs me. If I don't get back there, they'll hurt her. So we're going to go now."

"You're safe here." She is a remarkable liar. Her pulse isn't even fast. She's not panicking. I realize with a start she isn't lying, or at least she doesn't think she is. "I promise. And I'm watching for Annie. I'll know if she's in trouble. I would never risk her."

"She's not yours to risk. She's my responsibility." I back us through the door, fast, look both ways down the hall. It's clear. Blank. Fluorescent lights' monotonous hum the only sound. Right, I should go right. "Where are we? Are we still in Chicago?"

"No, we're in St. Louis."

I swear. That'll take longer. But as soon as I get out, I can call

James and tell him (he knows, he has to know that I didn't do this, it wasn't my idea) and I'll email Adam and get back and Annie will be safe and I have no plans at all until something works to give us a way out.

"Sofia," she says as we walk, body to body, around a corner. There's a door with one of those small brown signs indicating it's a stairway. This place looks like an old office building, but no one is here. "I want to help you."

"Generally I prefer my help not to come in the form of being attacked, knocked out, and thrown in the back of a van."

She laughs. Why is she laughing? She's crazy. "You'll have to excuse our caution. After our last encounter with you, we thought it best to talk in a controlled environment."

(Control, control, control. Control got Clarice killed.)

(Control didn't get Clarice killed. I killed Clarice.)

"How's that working out for you?" I say. I look behind my shoulder again—Cole isn't following us, that's bad, I'd know where he was if he were following us. Then the door to the stairwell opens and I pull back against the wall, press the pin against her neck.

And Adam—big smile, gray eyes, soft fingers, gentle Adam, safe and hiding in Chicago Adam—walks out into the hall.

He actually smiles when he sees me—his first reaction is to smile, what is wrong with him? I am so shocked that I drop my hand. I don't want him to see what I would have done to this woman, don't want him to see my hands any more than he already has.

"Fia!" He closes the few feet between us with his arms out and I tense (I don't want to hurt him, I never wanted to hurt him), and then he wraps his long arms around me in a hug. And my head doesn't scream *wrong, wrong, wrong*.

Oh, Adam. When will you stop messing everything up? And why do I keep letting you?

FIA

Sixteen Months Ago

~

"HOW CAN SOMEONE WHO SPENDS SO MUCH TIME IN the sun still have such pasty skin?"

I roll my eyes at Eden. "It's called porcelain. And sunscreen is my best friend." I love this soft white chair. I love this huge, smooth boat. I love the ocean. I love the wind and the waves and the spray. There is nothing out here. There is nothing to do. And since there is nothing out here and nothing to do and only James or Eden or the small, deliberately anonymous crew to talk to, there is nothing to make me feel sick and wrong.

Or at least only a little bit. Because there is still the tap tap tap. It never quite goes away. And the wrong feeling, too, but now it's a gentle hum and I can pretend like it isn't there. Pretending is another way of lying, and I am so good at both.

"Girls," James says, coming from the main cabin onto the deck where Eden is writing a letter to Annie and I am doing nothing, because nothing, nothing, nothing is my favorite. "Are you ready for an adventure?"

I sit up. Eden does, too, casually shifting in her bikini, stretching her legs. I wonder what she feels from him. I don't like it. I wonder if she feels that I don't like it from me. I decide to feel nothing, instead. "An adventure?"

"I think we've had enough of the open ocean and tiny islands. Time to begin the official study abroad section of your schooling. Or, really, time to club our way through Europe."

I raise an eyebrow. "Clubbing? Really? Do I strike you as the dancing type?"

"You strike me as exactly the dancing type. You just don't know it yet."

Eden jumps up, stretches her arms over her head, the tiny jewel piercing her navel winking an invitation in the sunshine. "Sounds good to me. As long as this adventure includes shopping, too?" She smiles hopefully. James nods and she turns to me and does a ridiculous, exaggerated victory shimmy.

I roll my eyes and snort. She's funny and beautiful. I wonder if we would have been friends in another world.

"See? Is that so hard?" Eden grins smugly and walks inside, and my accidental smile turns into a scowl.

"Did we have to bring her?"

James throws himself on the lounge chair next to me, putting an arm over his face to shade it from the sun. "Yes, we did."

"Why? She's obnoxious."

"Because," he says, reaching over and taking my hand from where my fingers are doing the tap tap tap on my thigh. "You tried to kill yourself, remember? So Eden had to tag along to make sure you didn't get that bad again."

I start to pull my hand back so I can cross my arms, but he keeps it in his, making a show of examining my fingernails. His fingers trace the inside of my wrist and something flares up inside me and, oh, I am so glad Eden is not here anymore.

James is the only person I can handle touching or looking at my hands. He knows everything they did. He doesn't care.

"Plus I am terrible at girl talk, and without Annie I figured you'd need someone."

This time I do yank my hand back. I hate that he brought up Annie. Because the thing about Annie is, I miss her, I do, I worry about her, but . . .

I also don't.

Being away from her for the first time in years is a huge relief. And I know she's safe because they have her and as long as they have her, they have me and for whatever reason they still want me. So Annie is safe. And she's alone and locked in that horrible prison of a school, and I am a terrible, terrible person for leaving her there.

But I don't have to look at her and know what I've done. I don't have to listen to her voice get gentle and soft and pierce right to the core of me and remind me, always remind me, of everything I've lost and taken. Of everything I still have to lose.

I know that Annie loves me no matter what, that she will always love me, and it is the very hardest thing of all to deal with. I do not want to be loved.

"At least you didn't bring a Reader. I hate them."

He laughs. "Me, too. You know the trick to Readers, though?"

"I swear in my head over and over again."

"That's a good one, but they get used to it pretty fast. If you can't focus on pissing them off, then always have a really obnoxious song going in the background of your brain. And if you need to make them feel so uncomfortable they stop listening, think about sex."

"Sex?"

"Sex." He is so beautiful I want to crawl across my chair and onto his and have him give me specifics to think about. But he is and has always been and will always be wrong, and I can't ignore that.

Can I?

"Should you really be giving me tips on how to bypass the people your father has spying on me?"

He smiles, and it's his sharp smile that I think he only uses with me. "You're my star pupil, remember? Just because you have to do what he wants you to doesn't mean you can't keep parts of yourself secret. It's about balance, Fia. Balance and patience and time."

"You've never struck me as the patient type."

He leans back, puts his arms behind his head, and closes his eyes. "Like I said. Secrets."

James was right. I love dancing. I love it so much I almost don't crave the alcohol being passed all around me, the drugs I see people taking. I almost don't wonder how much better the dancing would be if I took something. When I'm really dancing, when I'm in the middle of a crowd in the dark with the pulsing lights and pounding beats, I can lose myself in a way that's easy to get back from.

I love it.

We're somewhere in Germany. I don't know where; I don't care. Eden goes out most days and sightsees. I sleep in our obscenely expensive hotel suites and wait for the clubs. James has meetings, makes sure I eat enough, and prods me to do the occasional "assignment" (learning how to operate pretty much any common tech platform, for instance), and then we go dance.

I send Annie postcards that Eden buys for me, since it doesn't matter what they look like anyway, and pretend like I'm the one visiting mountains and castles and historic squares. Annie will like that. I hate that someone else has to read them to her, though. I hope it isn't Ms. Robertson.

"You aren't going to get ready?" Eden asks, eyeing me as she puts on another coat of lip gloss.

"Shoes. Skirt. Top. Ready."

"I mean, let's do something with your hair. Put it up. Twist it. And you could rock more makeup. You're not really selling it."

"What am I supposed to be selling?"

"Guys are pretty hot for you at these; I can feel them out for you, if you want."

"Do I strike you as particularly lusty?" I lay my emotions open, imagine them washing over her. I am the ocean we lived on for two months. I am empty. I am nothing.

"Stop it. You're so creepy." She stalks out of the room, muttering about missing Annie, and I smile.

Later I'm in the middle of the floor, lost, when someone takes my arm. I open my eyes, surprised to see James grinning at me. I'm shocked. He's never come to dance with me before. I move closer to him, excited, but he shakes his head and pulls me away toward the bar.

"I've got a game for you."

"A game?" I don't want to play a game. I want to dance. I want to dance with James. He's always finding little reasons to touch me—a hand at the small of my back, a flimsy excuse to take my hand in his and look at it—but he's never done more. I want more. I don't know what I want from him, exactly, just that I always want more.

"Do you see that guy over there at the bar?" He points to a barrel-chested man, midtwenties, nice clothes designed to show off how nice they are.

"Yes."

"Steal his phone, bring it to me, and then get it back to him without him noticing."

"That is the worst game I've ever heard of."

"I want to see if you can do it. I need five minutes with his phone. And then I'll dance with you." He smiles, his best, broadest, biggest manipulator of a smile. He doesn't use that smile on me. Until now.

"What makes you think I want you to dance with me?" I turn, angry angry angry. Fine. He wants a phone? I'll get him a phone. I pull back against the *wrong* buzz, disconnect from it, focus on this. Phone. I need that phone.

My hips take on a life of their own as I weave through the room. I pretend I am walking on the boat (I loved the boat) and let my memories sway the room for my alcohol-free brain.

"Josef, there you are!" I laugh and wrap my arms around from him behind, let them wander like a drunk girlfriend's might. "Have you been hiding from me?"

He turns (mean eyes, he has mean eyes, but his eyes aren't mean toward me right now) and smiles, bemused.

I take a drunken step backward, let my mouth form an O. "You aren't Josef." I giggle. It grates on my ears; it is a horrible sound.

"No." He smiles and I shrug.

"Too bad. You're cuter than he is." And then I do my hips-sway-because-I-am-drunk-and-think-I'm-sexy walk, and I know it will be no problem to come back when James is done and stand too close to not-Josef's side and slip back the phone I have in my hand.

It isn't. The whole thing is done in under seven minutes.

James beams at me when I walk back to him, so proud of my skills. I realize with a sinking click that I will earn my way the rest of this trip, exactly like Eden. It is not a vacation after all, not about making me better, not about James actually caring. Just more games, this time in the real world.

James holds out his hand. His black button-up shirt is undone at the throat. Even his throat is handsome, and I want to run my finger down it, down to the hollow at his collarbone. "Ready to dance?"

"Like I said. What makes you think I want to dance with *you*?" I turn and push my way back into the sea of bodies and try to lose myself. Alone.

ANNIE
Tuesday Afternoon
～

THIS IS THE FIRST TIME I'VE VISITED FIA'S NEW apartment, the place she's lived since she got home. But she never really came back to me. Just like I knew she wouldn't when I let her leave with James.

They've never let me visit here. Fia has to come to me, and only when they say she can. She's unpredictable, and I'm their insurance policy. They won't risk her snatching me and running off. I can't even leave the school building when Fia is in town; it's only when they have her elsewhere doing who knows what that Eden can take me out. With an escort, of course.

They didn't count on Fia being the one to disappear alone. I know she's scared, but I wonder . . . maybe she's better off.

I climb out of the car, Eden waiting to put my hand on the crook of her arm.

"She'll be okay," Eden says. "You'll find her."

"Soon," James adds, and his is less a comfort and more a threat. I hate him.

If I were Fia, if I were anyone else, I could get away from him now, run to someplace new, be free. But that's a lie. Because even if I could see, I couldn't leave without Fia. And if I ran, I'd do it knowing I would never really be safe, that no matter where I was, if I was still alive, Keane would somehow find me. My thoughts would never be safe. Not even my future would be my own.

He'll do whatever it takes to find Fia. If I do find her, it will be to save her from captivity and deliver her right back to it. Maybe we'll never get away. Our delusional plans not to plan will never work. We will never have an opening. There is nowhere for us in the whole world that Keane can't reach out to and drag us back from.

The world grows quieter as we pass through a door, sealing us into climate-controlled warmth and away from the mad, windy rush of the city. We go silently up stairs and James unlocks a door. I walk into an apartment with a hardwood floor. The air smells and tastes clean. Lifeless. But there's a hint of stale perfume somewhere that I can't place. Fia would never wear it.

"What does it look like?" I ask. I want to know where Fia has been living. I wish I could have visited her here. Lived with her here. "How did she decorate it?" I hate depending on someone else to tell me.

James answers. "She didn't. She said it was all the same to her."

"Where's her room?" In all honesty I have no idea if this will help me see her, but I had to feel like I was doing something other than sitting around, starving myself, trying to have a vision. Surrounded by her here, where she was the most, might help. I can force the visions sometimes, but it isn't easy, and usually it's only a snatch.

"Walk straight forward. You'll go through a short hallway. The door's open."

"You want me to come with?" Eden asks, but I shake my head. I'm glad James doesn't try to escort me there, either. I wish he weren't here at all. I hate that he knows her apartment, that he knows the Fia who lives here and I don't. I trace a hand along the wall, past the doorframe, into her room.

And this feels better, because it smells like Fia. It smells like spice and energy and vanilla. I take another step forward and trip on a pair of shoes in the middle of the room.

There's my Fia, too.

I shuffle carefully now, wading through clothes discarded on the floor, until I bump into the bed. The blankets are shoved and twisted around the end; I crawl on and push my face into her pillow. Fia, where are you? I miss your tapping fingers and your crazy laugh and all the things about you that I don't know.

I'm sorry I wanted you to be who you were before. I know you can't be her anymore. Come back to me and I'll help you figure out who to be now. Come back to me and I'll stop trying to fix anything and I'll just be your sister. I smash my face farther into her pillow, the pressure against my eyes creating a false sensation of light.

No, not false.

I'm seeing. I don't move, don't even dare to breathe. Fia. I want to see Fia. Show me Fia.

I see a man in a suit; he's older, his hair shot through with gray. He's at an imposing desk, with windows behind him. Outside is so white with snow the light is overwhelming. The room is strange—the walls curve, there are no corners. It's circular. On the floor the carpet has a design of some sort of bird, and there are flags, too, displayed prominently. I notice the same bird carved into the desk, and on one of the flags.

The man stands and holds out his hand, smiling. Another man, blandly handsome in an equally nice suit, takes it.

"Thank you for coming on such short notice." The first man walks over to a pair of plush couches, obviously at ease.

The second man sits across from him. "Of course, Mr. President. How is Lauren? I saw her on the way in."

The president laughs. "Best staffer we've ever had. Thanks again."

I want to throw up.

Because I know the second man's voice. For all his paranoia about not being seen, Keane neglected to take into account my memory for voices. Keane. It's Mr. Keane. He is flesh and blood, after all, not a monster behind his voice. And he is friends with the president.

Suddenly the images shift, swirl. I am dizzy with motion sickness, and if I weren't lying down, I would have fallen. Adam? It is. He's outside, walking.

Fia is with him.

He says something. I can't hear him because it's too windy, but Fia laughs. Really laughs. Not her James laugh, not her hollow-girl laugh. An actual laugh. And Adam looks at her in a way that is tender and hopeful and happy and innocent. I cannot imagine this is a way anyone who knows her looks at my sister.

Fia smiles.

They buy hot dogs from a street stand, and walk without purpose—Fia always has a purpose—while Adam talks so animatedly that he sends relish flying through the air and then blushes and apologizes. I don't know where they are, I can't figure it out. There's a strange silver semicircle dominating the sky behind them, and it's green and clean around it.

They sit on a bench. I suddenly feel as though I am eavesdropping on something I shouldn't, that I am invading my sister's privacy. Adam angles closer to her, his knees bouncing with nervous energy. She listens to him with her head tilted, but her eyes look faraway. He reaches out slowly and puts one of his hands over hers.

She stares at their hands like she can't understand what is happening. I expect her to pull back, to start tapping on her leg in the way she can't help. She doesn't. And then she smiles, and her smile breaks my heart because I can see in it that her heart is broken, too, but maybe it can be fixed here.

I open my eyes to my own familiar blackness.

"Did you see her?" James asks.

"Yes," I whisper.

"Where is she?"

I could tell him. I could describe it. The strange silver arch was huge. Surely it's distinctive enough to get a location from. I don't know when they'll be there, but they will, soon. Fia will be there, and we could get her back.

But if we don't, I think she might actually have a chance at being happy.

But if we don't, Keane has made it perfectly clear how much value my life has to him.

I sit up straight. For once in my life I have the chance to protect and take care of my sister. She gave up everything to do the same for me. I can give it up for her, too.

"She's in a cell somewhere. I have no idea. It looked permanent."

"Doris?"

I freeze, my heart stops. How could I not have heard Ms. Robertson come in? The perfume. She was already here. She was here all along. She can't know. She can't have heard.

"She's lying. She knows where Fia is. There was something about . . . what was it? Silver, huge, up in the sky but on the ground, too . . ."

I will not think of it. A song. I need a song. Fia sings songs. I will not think of it; I cannot think of it; I will not think of it.

"A pillar," James says. "A statue. A skyscraper. A blimp."

Don't say it, I think, don't say it.

"A sculpture. An airplane. An arch."

My mind snaps; I don't think the word but it's enough. Doris lets out a derisive laugh. "That's it. She didn't want you to say that one. A huge silver arch."

"St. Louis. I need ten men. We'll leave immediately."

"Want me to put any Seers on it?"

"No use. Annabelle's the only one who can see Fia well, and she's already done her job. Thank you, Doris. That will be all."

"I'll go order dinner," Eden says softly, squeezing my shoulder. "You feel like Thai? We'll do manicures, and tomorrow . . ." Her voice breaks a little. I know she hates Fia, but she feels what

I feel. She knows. "Things will be better. See you at home."

I hear them leave, numb with despair. My own traitor thoughts have destroyed my sister.

"You should have just told me," James says. "You make it so hard."

"Please, James. Please. I saw her. And she was happy. Or she could be, at least. She was out, away from all this. You say you care about her. Let her stay out."

"What about you? You know what it means if she doesn't come back."

"It doesn't matter. She deserves a chance. Please don't take it away from her."

There's a pause. It's long, too long. Then he says softly, thoughtfully, "How do you know she was happy?"

"She laughed. Really laughed. And she let him hold her hand."

"Him?" His voice is hard. I sink back into the bed. I have done it again. I have said the wrong thing and lost whatever chance I had. "She was with a guy? Who was he?"

"Please. Let her go. We can both let her go."

He snarls. "None of us gets out, Annie. We are all too steeped in blood for that." And then, when I am flinching for his next battery of words, he surprises me by sounding sad. "You said Adam Denting was bigger than you and Fia. So is what I'm doing. And I can't let her go."

I remember what Fia told me, about who the real Keane behind the school was. "What would your mother say?"

"That's just it. Nothing. Because she got out and left the rest of us here to deal with this mess. Now get up. I'm taking you back."

I will never get away, and Fia will always be dragged in because of me.

ANNIE

Six Months Ago

~

I AM TRYING TO FIGURE OUT HOW TO SEE.

So far, the information I've found out by being friendly and listening when I'm not supposed to is limited. Mostly things I already know. The school isn't a school so much as a testing ground for psychic talent. Only girls, too. I thought they might have an equivalent place for boys, but for whatever reason, boys can't do any of these things.

Which means thoughts and feelings are safe around security guards. It's something.

Girls are quickly weeded out for not being skilled, thus the reason the classes get so small so fast. Those who have strong enough abilities are slowly but surely sucked in, and those who can be trusted are moved up and out to do who knows what for Keane.

They never come back.

Those of us who are on shaky ground are kept here, in the massive school building, but away from the new students. They find what they need to threaten us with so we have no option but to work for Keane. Readers and Feelers are more common and seem to do better. Seers he doesn't trust. None have as much power or as high a place as Clarice did.

No one is like Fia, who can't do what we can but somehow is even more interesting to him than the rest of us. I know Fia's special, but I still can't understand why they care so much about her. Why they forced her to stay. Why they didn't do anything to her after she killed Clarice.

All the girls are found through rumor or odd news articles, occasionally through visions, then approached the same way I was—a scholarship, a prestigious school, specially tailored instruction for specially gifted girls. Then gradually the girls figure it out, learn they aren't alone, that they're surrounded by others who have the same gifts (or curses, depending on how you view it), given instruction and help and a home.

It's brilliant, really. The applications for espionage, both in business and in politics, are endless. Nearly all the girls start here so young and are treated so well that of course they want the power and money that is offered.

But knowing this all is not enough. It's not enough for me to keep Fia safe, for me to get her out of here. So I work on the only advantage I have, and that's seeing.

Clarice didn't teach me much. She told me to focus, but she always had me focus on Fia. I don't need to see Fia right now, though I want to, so much. If only to see whether or not she's happy. Her letters make her feel even farther away. They have no soul.

I've occasionally been able to get tiny flashes, glimpses of things I've thought very hard about, like the mountains where we used to live but that I don't remember from before I lost my sight. They had fewer trees than I imagined, more rocks. Beautiful. And then there are the strange ones, jumbles of images I can't sort through or make sense of.

So now I am fasting and staying awake as long as I can. Maybe if I push my body to the brink, push it as far as I can, my brain will take over and I'll be able to see more.

It works—sort of. I sit, so tired I can't think straight and so hungry my whole body is trembling. And then I see things.

Fia, on a balcony, with haunted eyes as she stares out at a city filled with stone buildings and winding streets. She looks healthy, if not happy. Healthy is something, at least. James is taking care of her like he said he would.

And then Fia dancing in the dark, the whole vision so filled with noise and movement I can barely figure out what is happening, but the way Fia moves I know in that moment she is free and it makes my heart ache.

A guy, so handsome my breath catches, with warm eyes and broad shoulders, sitting at a polished wood desk, staring at a picture of an older woman who has his same eyes. His whole face is a mask of anguish, and I wonder who he is, who she is. I don't see guys very often. Then I hear a voice—Fia's!—call out, "James? Are we doing this or not? The sooner we steal your crap, the sooner I get to dance."

James.

His face immediately resets itself into a calculatedly careless smile as he sets the picture facedown and stands.

It shifts and I see Eden, reading a book by a pool, looking up with an inscrutable expression as Fia walks by with James.

It shifts again and I see a guy, dark hair, his back to me as he stares at some sort of image of—what? It's black and white, see-through with light behind it—and traces his finger along it. I wonder who he is, but then my vision twists and I see a woman in an office. She mutters something to herself and I recognize Ms. Robertson's voice. It's evening, almost dark outside the window, and there is a half-empty bottle of something in front of her. She pours another tiny cup full, splashing some over the side, and drinks the whole thing in one shot. Then she puts the bottle back into the bottom drawer of her desk.

There is a small rolling suitcase on the floor next to her desk, unzipped, with unfolded clothes half spilling out.

And then my world is black again. What can I do with that?

What can I do with any of that? At least now I understand why so many of the women here fall all over themselves for James. But he's much more than he lets them see. Fia seems . . . stable. Not happy but stable and healthy looking.

I miss Eden fiercely. I wish I were with her. No idea who the guy was or what he was looking at.

Ms. Robertson will at some point in the near future drink herself into a stupor. Not very professional, and I don't see any advantage there.

Unless . . . she's gone right now. On a recruitment trip. I stand, almost fall as my head spins, and stumble to the hall. "Darren?"

"Yes, Miss Annabelle. What do you need?"

"I need to talk to Ms. Robertson. When does she get back?"

"Tomorrow afternoon."

"Okay, thanks."

I go back into my apartment, a smile on my face. Between my mattresses, hidden where Fia couldn't find them, I have an emergency stash of her old pills. The prescription was strange—it would knock her out, but you could wake her up and she'd be almost lucid. It was the only time I could get her to talk to me.

I didn't like what she said, but I heard things she'd never tell me otherwise. It's how I finally found out what Clarice made her do that day on the beach.

I tap out four pills into my hand. My security-free route to my daily walk around the interior courtyard of the building goes right past Ms. Robertson's office . . . and her desk with a drawer hiding a bottle of alcohol she'll be drinking out of tomorrow.

I knock on the door. No answer. Please, please let it be today that I saw. I push the door open.

"Ms. Robertson? Are you in here?"

A soft snore greets me. I smile and close the door behind me. "Doris, wake up."

No response.

"Doris!"

Her breathing changes and I hear her chair creak; a bottle or glass shatters against the floor.

"Whoopsie," she slurs. "Annabelle? 'Zat you?"

"Yes. I wanted to talk to you. About Sofia."

"Sof-ya. Glad she's gone. Hated her thoughts. Bad things. Always bad things."

"Why does Keane want her? Shouldn't he have gotten rid of her after she killed Clarice?"

Ms. Robertson snorts loudly. "Clarice got what she had coming. Told her, I told her, but she was always right. Going to be the first Seer that Keane promoted to his personal aide. Nobody was sad to see her gone. She was brutal."

"Was she going to kill me?" I ask. My heart is in my throat.

I've wondered, for so long. Was Clarice the one who was going to kill me? If she was, all Fia did was kill a killer. It would change everything.

"Who knows? You wouldn't've been the first. She hated you, too."

I frown, hurt. I always thought Clarice liked me. She was kind to me, helped me figure out my visions. "She did?"

"Hated any other Seers. Satota—satoba—sabotaged them. Didn't want anyone else Keane could depend on. I say the lot of you are pointless. Everything's always changing, can't see what you're supposed to, blah, blah, blah. Now reading, that's different. That's a real *skill*. But do I go anywhere besides this school with thoughts floating all around me, battering me, pounding in my skull? No. Do I get sent to a CEO or a senator? No. I have to live with teen whining all day every day. If I weren't putting three of my own ungrateful kids through school, I'd leave in a heartbeat. A heartbeat, I'm telling you. I'd leave. Leave."

She trails off, and I hear a soft thud against wood. Her head on the desk, I think. CEOs and senators. Is that where the other girls are going? Working for important people, stealing the very thoughts out of their heads?

"But what about Sofia? Why is she so special?"

"'Snothing. She can't make a wrong choice. Perfect instincts or intuition or whatever. Stocks, fighting, picking out liars, tricking people. Almost invisible to Seers, too, 'cause she's always changing and switching around." She snorts a harsh laugh. "Whole thing's silly. What good're perfect instincts on a crazy girl?"

"She's not crazy," I hiss.

"She's—wait, what're you doing in here? I can't hear you so well. Mebbe I had too much this time." Or *mebbe* the pills I added to your bottle yesterday were a bad combination.

"Go to sleep, you old bat." I turn and walk out of her office. Tracing my hand over the wall, I'm troubled. So what if Fia has perfect instincts or intuition? Why does that make her so valuable?

Then again, if you had someone who could make the best choice in any given situation, turn anything to her favor—if every gut feeling you had, every reaction you gave was always exactly right—the possibilities were even more intriguing than a Reader or a Feeler or Seer could offer.

But what Ms. Robertson had said still bothered me. Fia wasn't crazy, she wasn't, but she had been pushed so far. What would that do to her instincts, to whatever it was in her that was so attuned to everything? How would it twist her intuition?

Clarice, dead on the floor, a snap decision on Fia's part.

Clarice! Clarice, evil Clarice, who would have killed me. I have to tell Fia. This will change things, I know it will. She'll feel better, she won't have to be consumed with guilt. I run down the hall, up the stairs, wait impatiently for the guard outside the residence wing to open the door for me.

In my room I feel the list of numbers by my phone. James gave me his before they left. I tried calling a few times, but Fia didn't talk, not really. It was too depressing to try and keep up a conversation all by myself.

I dial and it rings and rings and I'm so nervous it'll go to voice mail I almost shout, then I hear James's voice. "Hello."

"James! I need to talk to Fia!"

"Annabelle? What's wrong?"

"Nothing! I need to talk to her."

"About what?"

I let out an exasperated breath. "About Clarice. She needs to know what I know."

"And what do you know?"

I'm too excited to lie. "Clarice was evil! We never knew if Clarice would have been the one to kill me, but I'm pretty sure it would have been her. And besides that, she did all sorts of other things. Even Ms. Robertson thought she was evil, and that's saying something. Where's Fia?"

There's a long pause, and I wait, buzzing, to tell Fia. But then it's still James on the line. "What do you think knowing this will change?"

"Everything! Fia doesn't have to feel guilty, she doesn't have to let it eat her alive!"

"I don't think you understand your sister. She didn't kill

Clarice because Clarice was evil. She killed Clarice to protect you. Clarice could have been Mother Teresa and Fia would have done the exact same thing."

"But . . . if she knew—"

"It wouldn't change anything. Fia made her choices based entirely on you, and it didn't matter who was on the receiving end of the death sentence. She chose you, Annabelle. Over Clarice. Over anyone. Even over herself. Nothing will change her feelings about what she did, because she knows she'd do it again. That's what she can't live with."

I drop onto the couch. "But she should know." It makes it better. It does.

"I think you're the only one whose guilt is eased by knowing about Clarice. Don't pretend it will help Fia. Now, she's sleeping and I hate to wake her. Is there a message you want me to deliver?"

"No," I whisper, and hang up the phone.

FIA

Tuesday Afternoon

~

I'M SITTING IN A LOBBYLIKE ROOM (FIRST FLOOR, two exits—one we came through, the other probably leads outside faster—five windows, freestanding chairs that can break a window or a head) on a couch with Adam. Sarah—brown hair brown eyes is named Sarah—brought me a cup of coffee, a muffin, and some aspirin. No one has a gun on me. No one is expecting me to run.

And . . . I don't feel like I should.

"Well, I'm confused." I lean back into the corner of the couch and tuck my feet up underneath me. I see Adam's eyes flick to my legs and then away as his face reddens because he is embarrassed he looked, and it is adorable. Also it makes me wish I had a longer skirt on. Or pants. Then he wouldn't have to be embarrassed. I want to be a girl he doesn't have to be embarrassed around.

I wonder what it would be like to be with a boy who blushes when he looks at my skin.

"I was confused when they found me, too," Adam says, grinning. He grins with his whole face. It's kind of beautiful.

"Yeah, about that. What happened to being dead?" I narrow my eyes and punch him lightly in the shoulder. "I want a refund. I gave you all my money."

"Oh!" He reddens further and stands up. "It's in my bag, I'll go—"

I roll my eyes. He's so sincere. "Kidding. Sit down. I didn't want you dead. This works, too, I guess. I just want to know how you got here. You had very specific instructions."

"We found him yesterday afternoon. I was watching very closely for him, and I saw him going to the Chicago library constantly to check his email."

Dumb Fia. DUMB. I can't believe I forgot to tell him not to plan anything and not to be predictable. Tap tap tap my finger on my bare leg, I am so glad he's not dead.

"So you guys weren't trying to kill him in that alley." I glance over at Cole (sitting in a chair—not close like Sarah but near one of the doors—watching the whole room like he isn't watching it). "Sorry about that."

He smiles, but, unlike Adam's, his is a lie and doesn't touch his eyes. "You didn't know. And you weren't the only one who drew blood." He looks pointedly at my bandaged shoulder, which still hurts but not as much as my head and my head is entirely my own fault.

"Lucky shot."

This time his smile does touch his eyes.

"So, what do you want with Adam?" I ask.

"We're very interested in his brain research. Why did the school want him dead? This seems like the exact thing they would be interested in, too. Right now they're hit-and-miss with finding girls, but if what Adam is working on pans out, it will give us a direct link to women with psychic abilities. It doesn't make sense for them to order a hit."

Because Keane wasn't behind the hit. Annie was. "Keane's going on advice from psychics. They aren't exactly reliable." I don't mean it as a dig against Sarah and cringe after I say it, but she nods.

"James Keane?"

I frown. "No. His dad."

"His dad?"

"Yeah, his dad. James isn't in charge."

It's Sarah's turn to frown. "You mean James doesn't run the school? He inherited it when his mother died, and we thought . . ."

Oh, perfect. They have no idea just how far and deep Keane's reach goes. They're still focused on the school. What about the stealing, the spying, the blowing people up? I don't have time for this. "I want to know who you are and why you're following James and looking for me."

Sarah crosses her legs and clasps both her hands around her knee. She has pretty hands, safe hands. "As you already know, I'm a psychic, or a Seer. When I was fifteen, a woman named Dayna Keane found me and invited me to attend her school. That night I had a dream that horrible things would happen if I went, so I declined. But I kept seeing the school and the changes there in visions. I've made it my goal to disrupt their operations, to rescue girls from them, and to prevent new girls from being manipulated. I think Adam can help me with that. And I'd like you to, if you will."

"How much good do you do?" They don't know nearly enough, but I want her to be real and honest and right. I want this to be true. But it doesn't feel right. It doesn't feel wrong, not the way the school always felt wrong wrong wrong, but it doesn't feel right. I don't feel sick, my heart isn't racing, I'm not falling. But I'm not . . . sure. If this was right, wouldn't I be sure? Wouldn't I know in my core? Wouldn't I feel that invisible something tugging me this direction?

"As much as we can," Sarah answers. "We're still trying to figure out exactly how far the school's reach extends. We don't know what their agenda is; we've never been able to track a girl once she leaves the school, though we suspect high-level placement through money and networking. We're focusing on prevention now, mostly. Keeping girls out to begin with."

"That's nice." I stand and walk to the window. It's a beautiful day outside. Clear and blue, and the trees have almost finished budding with new green life. The street is wide and lined with other blank office buildings and the odd chain restaurant. "Can I leave?"

"What?"

"Right now. Can I leave? Can I walk out the door?"

Sarah's voice is soft. "Do you want to?"

"I'd like a hot dog. Adam? Will you go for a walk with me?" I turn and look at him and hope. Hope that a boy like Adam will go for a walk with a girl like me.

"Oh, uh, sure." He stands, sticks his gentle hands in his pockets.

"Would you like a jacket? And shoes?" Sarah asks. I smile and nod. She takes her own off and hands them to me. The jacket is black and warm. The shoes are too big but only just. She is really going to let me walk out. Free and clear. With her prize Adam, no less.

I think it's all true. Everything she said.

Adam and I walk down the street; the breeze is cool but the sun is delicious. Adam tells me how he was so scared when Cole walked up behind him in the library that he tripped over his chair and fell in a huge heap and the librarian got mad at him.

I laugh. It doesn't feel like a lie bubbling out of my throat.

We buy hot dogs and they are disgusting but it was our choice to buy them. Adam talks nervously and quickly about where they're going. Sarah moves around a lot, but she said there's a bigger, permanent house with lots of medical research equipment. I like the way he gestures, forgetting his hands are full and flinging relish from his hot dog onto the sidewalk. Other normal people doing normal things pass. I steal a phone out of someone's pocket (I feel like I should have a phone), and we find a bench on the edge of the grassy area surrounding the arch. It's huge and silver, dancing through the sky, and I cannot tell if it is taller than it is wide or wider than it is tall.

I tap tap tap on my leg because I am not sure what I am supposed to be doing.

I am not sure.

Nothing is right or wrong here. How am I supposed to make a decision when nothing is right or wrong?

". . . and they're getting funding for new MRIs in hospitals around the country so we can run tests. With real-world data, I could do so much." His voice gets faraway and dreamy. I laugh. I am sitting next to a cute boy on a bench and he is dreaming of MRIs and research data.

He smiles, and then he reaches out and takes my hand. I look at our hands, together. He has seen some of what my hands can do. He is still touching me. "Fia, I . . . I think you should stay. You don't have to go back. Ever. You never have to work for this Keane again. We'll figure out a way to get your sister out, and you can both stay with us, with Sarah and the Lerner group. We could help so many people."

I can see it. I can see a happy life with a happy boy. I can see the person he thinks I am when he looks at me—this wonder, this strong and brave and strange girl. He is half in love with his idea of me, and if I stayed . . .

Maybe I could heal. Maybe I could turn back into the sister Annie wants me to be. Maybe I could leave the last five years behind me and never have to think about them again. Never have to be that girl again. Maybe, maybe, maybe I could really be loved by someone like Adam.

That would be nice. And easy.

I can't feel, though. There is no right or wrong. What am I supposed to do when there is no right or wrong?

I look at our hands again and I know my hand doesn't fit in his like it should. Someone else's will. Someone else whose hands aren't impossibly broken. Someone else whose soul isn't impossibly broken.

But I want to pretend to be her.

I take my hand out of Adam's, smile at him, and I don't know if the smile is a lie or not. "I'm going to walk around for a little while. To think. I'll meet you back at the building, okay?"

"Okay," he says, and his eyes, his mouth, his words are hope.

As soon as he is gone I pull out the phone and dial Annie. It rings and rings and I tap tap tap and no one answers. I dial James. It rings and he picks up.

"Who is this?"

"Is Annie okay?"

He swears, and it makes me feel homesick. "Fia? Where are you? We know you're in St. Louis. Give me a location."

"Is Annie okay?"

"She's fine. I wouldn't let anything happen to her."

"Bring her with you."

"What?"

"I'm not going to do anything unless I can see that she's with you and she's safe. If I see you here and she's not with you, I'll disappear forever. You know I can."

"Fia, please."

"Please nothing. Do you know what they're offering me? They're offering me *me*. Free. Whatever, whoever I want to be."

He is quiet and I wonder what his face looks like right now, whether he can still feel my lips on his like I can feel his on mine. "You can't have that."

"I could."

"No, you can't. You don't get to choose that. I need you."

"You use me."

"I—yes. I use you. I need to use you. I can't let you go; I can't do this by myself."

"I think we both know you are never by yourself." The words come out stinging and petty and I hate hate hate the jealousy ringing in my voice.

"That's not what I mean. I need your help. You aren't like whoever these people are. You can't just get out, pretend like none of this happened, pretend like you aren't so far gone you can't ever go back."

"I won't help your father anymore," I say, and I know it's true.

"I'm not asking you to help my father. I'm asking you to help me. Why do you think I've trained you to lie, to cheat the Readers and the Feelers and the Seers? Do you really think I am working *for my father*, the man who destroyed my mother? The man who destroyed you? Is that what you think of me?" He sounds hurt.

"I don't know what to think of you." I close my eyes, squeeze them shut, try to clear my head. I have too many feelings for and about James. "I could help people here. They're going against your father. I could help them."

"They're barely scratching at the farthest parts of his reach. They know nothing about what's going on. Do you really want to help?"

I wish he were here so I could see him to know if he's lying. But he's right about Sarah and Lerner, I know he is. She's too happy, too calm. She doesn't understand anything about what's really going on. She hasn't seen anything. "Yes. I really want to help."

"Then help me destroy my father from the inside. You're the only one who can. I've been building toward this for years. *Years.* I need you, Fia. I can't plan things, I can't decide things because if I do, one of his Seers might see. But they can't see you. I've wanted to tell you so many times, when you'd ask me why I was working for him. It killed me that you think I'm like him. I want you to—*I want you.* I always have. But I couldn't be sure, couldn't know if you'd agree. For this to work, no one can know. They can never suspect I am anything but loyal and that you are totally mine."

I look out at the trees, at the perfect blue of the sky. I am untethered. I am on my own track. I am no one's.

No. I am still Annie's. I will always be Annie's. And as long as she is out there, she isn't safe, and as long as she isn't safe I can do nothing but protect her. I will always be tied to that path, to those choices, to those instincts. Even if I get her away, even if Lerner can somehow help us, Keane won't stop looking for me. Annie will always be in danger because she will always be the only way to control me.

"We don't get to choose happy," James says, and I know now that he isn't lying. That he's talking to me in a way he won't talk to anyone else, not ever. Because James and I speak the same language. He has lived a lie with every move and every choice and even every thought and emotion for years now. "You and me. I wish we could choose happy. I wish I could let you go. But I need you. Please don't walk away."

I look down at my hand, remember the way it looked in Adam's. Think about the other life I could have. Think about how I don't feel anything now, right or wrong, right or wrong, I could go either direction and neither is right or wrong. "Bring Annie with you. Tomorrow. Underneath the arch at noon."

I hear a soft exhalation on his end. I picture his face. I think he is relieved and a little sad at the same time. "You're still with me. Thank you."

"Just bring Annie." I hang up.

Tomorrow I will be free. Really free. Forever.

FIA

Six Months Ago

~

IT'S BEEN ALMOST A YEAR.

I have taken laptops, sneaked into offices, cracked safes, and gotten James into places he shouldn't have been. I have been his "date" at political functions, at luncheons with other rich worthless people, at club after club. I have danced and sabotaged and stolen my way across Europe, and I have no idea what any of it was for. I follow instructions and turn off the part of my brain that works for myself. Off, off, off. It's easy, really.

I am happiest and most miserable with James. Sometimes I think I love him. And sometimes I think I hate him more than anyone else in the whole entire world, because he brought me back from the darkness where I tried to end myself, but I do not know this me that has taken my place. He is kind and he is funny and he is angry and he lies with everything he is.

Nearly a year without Annie. Annie, who I was never apart from our entire lives.

She writes me, but her letters are all false cheer. In one she "decided" not to go to college because she couldn't find a program she liked, and the Keane Foundation was "kind" enough to let her stay on. At the end of every letter she tells me she's still planning not to plan and can't wait not to plan with me again.

Today's letter leaves me feeling hollow. I read it again and again, but it only makes it worse.

"Hey," James says, leaning his head into my room. This Paris hotel is old in the way that it's good to be old, apparently, and smells like money and dust. My bed is massive (I drown in it, and it doesn't matter how big the bed is, my nightmares more than fill it) and four-postered and cold. I'm sitting in the middle of it, reading the words.

"I knocked," he says. Then he walks in and sits next to me. "What's wrong?"

"I don't remember this. At all. I don't even know the girl she's talking about."

He takes the letter from my hands, reads it. It tells a story about Annie and Fia when they were little. Fia's seventh birthday. Their parents taking them on a hike in a canyon near their home in the Colorado mountains (I remember the mountains,

I do, they made me feel safe, I want the mountains back), where they had put together a treasure hunt, but their mom had unknowingly hidden half the clues in poison oak and within minutes they were all covered in bumpy itchy horrible rashes.

So they drove home, the mother crying and the dad laughing because he said it was the only thing he could do, and then the mom laughing so much she was still crying. According to Annie, Fia wasn't sad, she was angry, so angry as she said, over and over, "I told you those bushes were wrong. I told you not to touch them. Now Annie's hurt. I TOLD YOU."

The letter said Fia knew even then what was wrong and right.

I am so filled with wrong I don't remember what right is. I am not that little girl. I don't want to be that little girl.

"You were young," James says. "It makes sense that you wouldn't remember it."

"I don't remember them. My parents, those people. When we had to move in with our aunt and she sold our house, it was like losing them all over again, and then when we came to the school and my whole brain, my whole soul, my whole every- thing was overwhelmed with this constant flood of *wrong*, how could I hold on to them? I don't remember them. My parents are dead and I don't remember them. And I'm trying to lose Annie, too."

"Fia, come on, you—"

"If that story is true, then it's my fault. If I could tell even then when something was wrong, then Annie isn't the one who should have stopped them from getting in the car that day. I am. But I don't remember—*I don't remember*—if I could feel anything or not. Everything is my fault."

I don't realize I'm crying until James wipes a tear from my face. He pulls me close, my head against his chest and his heart is steady, steady, steady. He can't lie with his heartbeat.

"It's not your fault."

"It is."

"Did I ever tell you about my mom?"

"She shot herself."

"She did. Did you know she started the school? Not how it is now. She wanted to reach out and help girls like her. Give them a place where no one doubted them or thought they were crazy. It used to be a very different school." He sounds almost wistful. I have never heard this from him. And I know he is not lying. "It was her whole life. She helped a lot of girls. Then my father got involved and shifted and twisted everything in that special way he does."

"Is that why she killed herself?"

"Yes."

"Then why? Why are you working for your father? All this information I'm stealing for him. What is it for?"

He tenses. "Have you talked with him or anyone about what we're doing?"

"No."

"Good. Don't."

"But, James. He destroyed your mother's school. He destroyed your mother. He destroyed *me*." Because this is my question, has always been my question, will always be my question. If James works for his father, how can I not want to destroy James, too?

"Don't do that," he says, taking my hand in his to stop the tap tap tap. "Please just be patient and trust me. I will always take care of you. I promise."

The wrong buzzes and fades and I want it to fade and I close my eyes and let him hold me. I let myself believe him. Because I don't want to take care of anyone anymore. Not even me.

The wind whips my hair around as James takes the corners too fast in the tiny convertible. The roads are narrow and winding, leading back from the Greek shipping baron's sprawling estate.

I wish I were driving. He taught me to drive and I am an excellent driver; I never want to be in the passenger seat again. But other than that, this moment is perfect. I laugh. "That was fun."

"It was. You were amazing, as usual."

"Expect nothing less. People are phenomenally stupid when it comes to smart phones."

"Well, seeing as how you accomplished in ten minutes what

I'd allotted two hours for, the rest of the day is officially yours. What would you like to do?"

"I want to take a nap. On the beach. And then I want to go dancing."

"Done and done."

The sand is blinding white and the water is an impossible turquoise. It makes me feel bad that I haven't looked more on all these trips, that I haven't absorbed it to describe to Annie.

Nope. No thoughts of Annie. I stretch out on my chair, let the sun soak me. It's been so much easier, turning it all off. And it works better, too. It's like back when they'd force me to fight. As soon as I'd give up and disengage my feelings, myself, I could go on pure instinct and everything made sense, everything was action-reaction with no thought necessary.

Being with James now is like that. I don't have to think. I don't have to feel. I put myself on the path he wants and just go. I'm not happy, but I'm not unhappy. I am perfectly nothing, and it is easy. James takes care of me.

"Should I call Eden to meet us?" he asks, pulling off his shirt (I love I love I love it when he does this). He's on a lounge chair right next to mine. They are touching. We are not touching, but we could be. He never touches me without a reason.

He is very, very careful. I wish he wouldn't be.

"Why on earth would we want Eden to meet us?" I ask.

"She might feel bad."

"Ah, but that's the glory of not being Eden. She can feel bad all she wants and we never have to feel it!"

"You, beautiful girl, are mean."

I smile and pull my sunglasses down. "You love me."

He laughs (I wish he hadn't laughed, why did he laugh?) and leans back into his own chair. The beach isn't crowded, but there are enough people to populate the rush of the bay with noise and laughter and it is all a happy, busy hum in the background.

I tap, tap, tap without urgency, because I am nothing and nothing matters.

"James? Is that you? I don't believe it!" A man's voice, with a trace of an accent I can't place. I don't sit up but turn my head to see an olive-skinned, dark-curly-haired guy around James's age laugh and raise his arms as though he expects James to get up and hug him.

"Rafael," James says, sitting up but not standing. Rafael slaps his hand on James's back.

"It's, what, two years? Where have you been?"

"Some of us have to work for a living, you know."

Rafael laughs, tipping his head back, his Adam's apple bobbing under a hint of dark stubble in the sun. Before he even looks my way I know he is wrong. Not dangerous wrong, but . . . potentially dangerous wrong. And there's something else. The way he stands over James, the way his smile is stretched to show all his teeth. He knew James would be here. This wasn't a chance encounter. But I don't think it's one James expected.

"And who is your beautiful friend? Is she—she isn't one of those girls, is she? The ones you told me about?"

James waves a hand dismissively in the air, but I see the lines of his shoulders, they are tight. He isn't happy, but you would never know from his voice. "I said a lot of things when I was drunk, Rafael. Which was pretty much all the time. You really believed my stories?"

"About women who can see into your head? Of course I did. It explains my ex perfectly. But you never answered who your friend is." He leans over James's chair to mine and I feel very vulnerable laid out in just a bikini, I want to stand, to get in a defensive stance, but I don't need to.

Not yet.

"Emilia," I say, and he takes my hand (he shouldn't touch my hand) and brings it to his lips.

"Charmed. So you cannot see the future or read my thoughts?"

"Judging by the way you're staring at my chest, I'm glad I can't read your mind." I sit up. (Well-muscled but in a carefully sculpted way. No practical use. I could snap his wrist.) I pull my hand away.

He laughs, turns, and slaps James's shoulders again. "I like this one. Is she yours?"

James shifts closer to me, puts an arm behind me, crossing the full length of my back. His skin is on so much of my skin, and he did it on purpose. "Yeah."

I lean my head on his shoulder and I can't help it, there is a smile blooming on my whole face, my whole body. I feel this smile, like I haven't felt anything in a very long time. I *am* his. I am.

Tonight I am going to dance with James. Tonight I am going to dance with him and he will kiss me, and we will be together. I don't care if there is the little wrong buzzing at the back of my head. I want this.

Rafael winks. "You always had the best taste. Come back to the yacht with me; it'll be like old times. You can share your good fortune."

Again Rafael smiles at me and he is wronger than wrong, but there is no danger here on this bright beach next to James. Still, my smile drops and my eyes narrow and I could break-snap-break him.

"We have other plans."

"Cancel them. You and I have things to discuss. So much to catch up on." Rafael has lost the false good-natured tone of his voice; it's brimming with intensity now.

James pretends not to notice Rafael's mood, waving a hand in the air as he leans back in his chair and pulls my head onto his shoulder, draping his fingers on the curve of my waist and it is nice, so nice, I think I have never been this happy.

Rafael slides back into a smile. "You know my number. And I know yours." He leaves and I do not move, will not move, not ever. Right, right, right. I will *make* this feel right.

"Sorry about him," James mutters.

"It's fine." I smile and close my eyes. It's better than fine.

I put my hair up. I take it down. I have no sense of how I should get ready tonight. Sometimes I get a feeling—one pair of shoes over another, one way of doing my hair—that for whatever reason is right. Tonight I can't get a read on those feelings. Everything is scattered and shattered and put back together.

Tonight I am going to dance with James.

I laugh, giddy, and leave my hair long and waving down my back. Simple. I'll keep it simple, because James has seen me through so much and I don't need to change, not for him, never for him. We understand each other. I can read the lines of his shoulders, catalog the lies of his smiles; he can touch my hands and not care.

I'm his. It's such a relief to be someone's, to not have to be my own (to not have to be Annie's—don't think about Annie, not tonight, especially not tonight).

It's still early, we aren't leaving yet, but I hold my shoes and dance and twirl barefoot out of my room and into the hallway of the cool white house we're staying in. It is all stone and tile and brilliant splashes of color. I dance past the hallway, past the kitchen. I am going to dance into pieces, I am ready to go, I am ready for tonight.

Laughter and hushed voices from the kitchen. Something is off, my stomach isn't giddy with butterflies so much as sick with them now, and I don't want to but I have to, I have to see.

I am a ghost, I am a whisper of feet on the tile. The arched entry to the kitchen shields me and I peer past the edge and there is Eden.

And she is wrapped around—wrapped around—wrapped around James, my James, and she is laughing and her hands (not my hands, not my horrible hands) are in his hair and she is whispering in his ear.

"I promised her dancing," he says, and she frowns.

"But I'm so tired of dancing. I'm lonely. I want to stay in tonight. With you."

"Another time, love," he says.

Love, love, love.

Love.

My dancing heart has danced itself apart and I was wrong, of course I was wrong, I am always wrong, everything is always wrong.

I am James's but he is not mine.

"Fia?" he calls, pulling away from Eden (soft Eden, untrained Eden, Eden with all her soft parts that I could hurt, hurt,

hurt—no, don't think about it, get away from Eden, don't let her feel it). "You ready?"

I back into the other room. My feet are ghosts and my heart is a ghost and my dreams? I have no dreams.

I am an idiot.

"I'm ready," I say. I wipe it clean, push it away, I am nothing, I feel nothing, there is nothing here.

Eden squirms when we get in the car. "She's doing that thing again."

"What thing?" James asks. He is smiling and driving, and I wish I were driving. I would drive us off a cliff. No I wouldn't. (Maybe I would. I am so stupid, I am sick with the stupidness of me.)

"That thing where she feels totally empty. It gives me the creeps. She hasn't done it in a long time."

"*She* is sitting right here." My voice is bright. My voice is a lie. I can lie better than you can, James.

"You're happy, right?"

"The happiest." I smile at him. I am going to dance tonight. I am going to dance tonight and I am not going to dance with James. I will never dance with James.

The club is the same as every other club we go into anywhere else in the whole world. Music and lights and bodies. I leave James and Eden without a word and go to the center of the floor and dance out my rage and my sorrow and dance out everything I am not.

I am not a girl who thought she was in love with James. I am not a girl who has failed and betrayed her sister at every possible turn. I am not a girl whose hands have ended lives. I am not a girl. I am just a body in motion.

"Emilia?"

I do not turn around until the hand comes down on my shoulder and I remember that today I was Emilia. I twist out from under the hand and turn to see Rafael. He is beautiful and he thinks I am beautiful and everything about him is slick and predatory—and he wants me.

He is wrong and I should not encourage him, I should leave right now and find James. This is not safe. (There are too many bodies, several of the tall, broad guys around us are obviously with him. I am outnumbered; it is dark; he thinks I am very young and very helpless and only one of those is true.)

He does not like James. He hates him. I noticed on the beach, but I was distracted by James claiming me. Not claiming me. Using me. Keeping me away from Rafael.

I smile and raise my arms over my head, dance closer to Rafael. He hates James. He is dangerous. I let him put his hands on my hips and twist my body against his. Because he is not James.

And James does not want me this way.

"You are beautiful," he whispers in my ear and he is not lying. I turn my back to him, trace my arm behind myself, onto his neck. We are dancing and dancing and then before I realize it he is kissing me.

It is my first kiss.

I want to cry. I want to sink into the ground and disappear. I want to be the nothing that I thought I was. His mouth is everywhere, his hands are everywhere, suffocating me, and I cannot breathe and I want to go home, but there is no home. I want Annie.

"Let's go somewhere else," he says, taking my hand in his and pulling me through the crowds. It is wrong, and I have counted the men with him and there are too many, and if James does not like him, then he must be a truly horrible person.

We walk out of the club into the dark night and the air is sharp with a humid, cold bite. I shiver and Rafael turns, wraps his arms around me, puts his mouth to mine again, pushes me up against the wall of the building. He is all tongue and hands and he disgusts me, but I disgust me, too.

Too wrong. I don't want this. I push him back, off me. "I'm going inside," I say.

"Come on, baby." He tries to come in close and I push him again. "Don't be like that." His voice isn't sweet like honey anymore. It is low and dark like tar. "Let's have some fun. We'll go to my boat and have some fun. And then we'll talk about my friend James."

"Thanks but no." I try to walk past, but the men with him (five and they move quickly and, unlike Rafael, they have muscles for a reason other than looking pretty, and I have no weapons) close the gaps, blocking me in.

"You *are* one of them. One of his girls. I've heard the rumors. And James has unfinished business with me. He's very bad at keeping promises, but maybe his girl is better." He has me back against the wall; he traces one of his fingers down my neck, down, down, down.

I knee him in the groin. "I'm nobody's girl."

He calls me a nasty name, and that annoys me because he has no right, and then one of the men grabs for my hair (I should have put it up). I duck, get low, kick at knees and elbow at noses. I want a knife. I have two down, three left, and now they are careful, wary. I have shown my hand.

I laugh. This is fun. This is what I wanted all along, I realize. This is better than the dancing. This is getting lost while doing something. I duck a rush, push the man so he careens forward and his head connects with the wall with a dull thud.

Someone grabs me around the waist and I slam my head back into his nose, hear it crack. He lets me go and I drop to the ground, sweep the feet of the only man left, propel myself to standing, and kick him in the face.

Rafael pushes himself up against the wall, and he does not think I'm beautiful anymore.

"You're crazy," he hisses.

"Too true."

"Fia!"

I turn and there is James, and he's furious. I've never seen him so angry. "What are you doing?"

"I was dancing." I shrug.

"James, you owe—" Rafael starts, but James hits him in the stomach so hard Rafael collapses.

"We're done here," James says to him.

I walk past them down the dark, empty street. I think I'll walk back to our house. It's only a few miles and I like the night air.

James grabs my arm and I know I don't have to elbow or kick, but I know where I need to if I want to. Want and need. Such a fine difference.

"What were you thinking?" he shouts.

"I wanted someone to dance with. He was a great dancer. Terrible kisser, though. And an even worse fighter."

"Fia!" He yanks my arm so hard I twist to face him. "You can't just—you have no idea who he is! He's dangerous—he could have hurt you. You of all people should have known that! Why would you take that risk?"

I glare at his face, his face that I have wanted for so long. "Sometimes I pick things that aren't good for me."

"What if something had happened?"

"I'm sure Eden would have comforted you."

His face freezes, then falls. "It's not like that. She—I have to keep her happy. That's all it is. I don't feel anything for her. The feelings she picks up off me aren't for her. Never for her. Let me explain."

"No, let me explain. You're right. I did know better than to go with Rafael. But I knew better about you, too. From the moment we met, you were wrong. You were always wrong. And I ignored it, and I pretended it wasn't true. I'd like to go back to Chicago now. You don't have to manipulate me, pretend to care, pretend to be my friend to get me to do what you want; I don't have any other choices. But I'm done playing make-believe."

He looks hurt. He looks like he wants to say something. He is a liar, liar, liar.

I will go home, and I will see Annie when they let me, and I will do whatever they say because I am not a person. Not anymore. James was my one hope for something more, but he was always, always a Keane.

Still, I will protect Annie. She is the only person in the world who loves me. She is the only person in the world who would never use me. She is my anchor, the chain around my ankle, the thing that means it doesn't matter what James does or who he is—I will still be his because I will always be Annie's.

ANNIE

Tuesday Afternoon

~

"WHO WAS THAT?" I ASK, POUNDING ON THE DOOR to my bedroom. How dare James lock me out of my own room to talk on the phone. I lean my ear close, trying to hear. "Was it Fia? Is she okay?"

He opens the door and I almost fall forward. He catches me, then leaves me standing there. I hear him opening and slamming drawers.

"What are you doing? Get out of my stuff!"

"You're coming with us to get Fia."

"She's okay." I slump against the doorframe with relief.

"For now. Either she already got away or she can at any time. Which you cannot tell anyone. The story is she's escaping tomorrow and coming right back. No one can know she thought about leaving forever. If they think they can't control her anymore through you, they have other plans. I won't let them do those things to her. We have to make them think she never even considered not coming back." He stops, swears. "You're useless around Readers. I'll have to leave Doris here and bring Eden. I'll tell them I'm taking you in case you have any more visions."

She's okay. She's okay. Then . . . why bring her back? "If she's okay, can't we—can't we just not find her? Please."

"That isn't an option. She knows it. You should, too."

Every part of me is heavy and tired. All the times I've tried to help Fia, protect her, I've failed. And the one time I went further than that, tried to protect more than us, all it did was backfire and push Fia further away. Adam is still alive and those women will still be found and destroyed. I thought I was doing something important for once, changing something for the better.

Maybe I can help in St. Louis. Maybe I'll see something and be able to use it. Maybe this will finally be our chance, being together far from here.

"Why are you bringing me?" I ask, suddenly suspicious. "Am I some sort of bait to force Fia back? I won't do it. If you take me in public, I'll scream bloody murder. I will *not* ruin her chance to be free."

"It wasn't my idea." He zips up a bag, then pushes past me. "I don't want to bring you any more than you want to come. But Fia said she would only meet me if she could see you with us."

"Then I'm not coming." I stand straighter, triumphant. If the only way I can be there for my sister is by not being there, then that's what I'll do. I don't care what they do to me. I'll figure out how to get away on my own, if I know that Fia is free.

"I don't have time for this," he snaps. "I need to be in St. Louis in case she calls again." My front door opens, and he shouts for Darren. I run into my room, lock it, then barricade myself in my closet. I won't. I won't go.

The pounding starts on the bedroom door, and I brace my feet against the closet. Then it's light, and I'm outside.

The air is heavy with humidity, the spring day almost oppressively warm. Everything has a sleepy, thick feel to it; even the buzz of a lawn mower nearby is muffled. I look and see two girls, the same height, their hair the same color. One is beautiful, her face haunted and innocent at the same time. The other is me.

I am seeing myself again.

We're next to some strange building, the narrow wall brilliant silver and going straight up into the sky. Green grass surrounds it and people who aren't in focus pass around us, not connected to us, not noticing us. I can't see anyone I recognize, but I know—I can feel—that we are being watched. Fia puts her hands out and takes mine. She's holding my hands!

She looks awful. She's in a black shirt that's too big for her, there's a bruise forming on one cheek, and she has nasty cuts on her arms. I look absolutely terrified.

"Fia," I say. My voice sounds strange, foreign. Like I am barely squeezing it out. "I'm so sorry. For everything. But it's okay. I understand." I smile and, though tears are streaming down my face, I keep smiling.

"Annie," she whispers. "It's the only way. I can't protect you anymore, and we can never be free. Not together. I'm so sorry, but it's the only way." She lets go of my hands; I keep them in fists at my side. Then Fia leans forward and kisses my forehead. She pulls out a knife that gleams as brilliant silver as the building. It glints in the sun as she holds it at her side. "I love you. I love you, but I need you to be dead. You have to be dead."

She brings the knife between us, and all I can see is our bodies, the knife somewhere in the middle, and her other arm behind me like she is hugging me. Then she steps back and the knife is red, so red, and I drop to the ground, my hands on my stomach.

I don't move.

I'm not moving.

Fia holds out the silver-red knife, looks down at it. "Goodbye, Annie. I love you." Then she turns and walks away.

And I am on the ground, and I am not moving, and I will never move again.

The door back in the darkness crashes open and someone grabs me roughly by the arms and yanks me out of the closet.

"Don't do this, Annie," James says. "We can make you come."

"Be careful with her!" Eden shouts. "Annie, what's wrong? She's freaking out."

"Of course she's freaking out, that's what she does."

I barely listen to James and Eden bickering about me. I can't go. If I go, Fia will kill me. Why would she do that? Why? Why after all this time? She kills me! She kills me! She . . .

She needs me to be dead. I've said it myself so many times: Fia can never be free because she will always have to protect me. As long as I'm alive, there will be a way to control Fia, to force her to do things she never would otherwise.

As long as I'm alive.

Fia needs me to be dead. I swallow hard, more scared than I have ever been my entire life. Except that night, the night Fia took the pills and I thought I'd lose her forever. Keane has made it clear that if Fia doesn't come back, I am as good as dead. I have no doubt his method will be far more horrifying and painful than hers. If this is the only thing I can ever do for her, if this is the only way I can protect her, like she's always tried to protect me, how can I not do it? She'd give up her future for me. She already did.

"It's okay, guys," I say, surprised by how clear and calm my voice comes out. Maybe I *can* lie, after all. "I'll come with you. It's fine."

It's fine. It's fine. It's fine. I will do this for Fia. It's finally my turn to take care of her.

FIA

Late Wednesday Morning

~

I SHOULD WEAR A BLACK SHIRT TODAY. I PULL ONE out of the small pile of clothes the Lerner group provided. Jeans. Shoes I can move in.

My hands tremble.

I finish lacing the sneakers when there's a soft knock. "Come in," I say, because I have never had rooms that keep people out anyway.

Adam opens the door and smiles shyly at me. "Hey. How are you?"

I stand and stretch my arms over my head, my stitches pulling and itching in my arm. I want to get them out. "I'll be good."

"I was wondering if I could . . . well." He reaches up and runs his long fingers through his hair. "This is more awkward than I thought it would be. But I was wondering if I could get an MRI of your brain and also draw some blood."

No. No no no. Never let them do that. Never let them find anyone else like you, not ever, not ever. I smile and shake my head. "I never let a boy see my brain until the third date."

His eyes go wide and then he laughs. "Sorry. I guess that was too forward."

"You at least owe me dinner and a movie first."

His smile hits me straight through, breaks my heart. "I'd like that."

Oh, I wish. I wish I were a girl for this boy to take to dinner and a movie. I could be, still. I could have that life. I could earn the way he looks at me. I glance at the clock. Almost time. Can't think. I pull out the tiny, pay-as-you-go phone I asked Sarah to buy for me. "Do you have a phone?"

He nods. "Are you going to throw it out another window?"

"No phones out windows today. Maybe something else. I need you to do me a favor. I need you to call this phone at 12:20." I give him the number. He'll do it, of course.

I slip the phone into my pocket next to my stolen one, then sit on the edge of the bed, pat the spot next to me. He sits. His feet stretch out onto the floor. "Adam, listen to me. I know about working for people who think they know more than you do. Promise me that whatever you do here, you'll be careful. Promise me you'll always listen to that thing deep inside you that tells you whether something is right or wrong. Even if it's just a twinge. Even if it's just a hint of a hint of a feeling. Because you could save—or destroy—a lot of lives. You're going to have help, though. Someone who really does know more than you do."

He smiles and looks at me with hope in his gray eyes. This boy is built of hope. What does that feel like? "I'm so glad you're staying."

"Thanks for looking at me like . . . like I could be whole. You have no idea what it means to me." I lean in to kiss him on the cheek and he surprises me by turning his head and our lips connect and he is soft and sweet and true, true, true.

I could have kisses like that for the rest of my life. Kisses that don't know who I am. Kisses that make me feel more and less than what I am. But my finger tap tap taps on my leg and reminds me that I am not who Adam thinks I am, and it makes me want to cry. It's not that I don't deserve his kiss. It's that the person I am can never really share a life, a soul, with the person he is.

He pulls back, looks down at the bed with a semicircle sweep of his lashes. "I'm sorry, I know we don't really know each other, but I've wanted to do that."

I sigh and glance at the clock; it's time. "Don't be sorry. I'm not. Thanks again. And don't forget to call."

He feels *right* for this. It'll be okay. I stand and walk out of the room, jog down the hall. Back to the lobby area. I'm in luck, Sarah and Cole and, oh, even better, Sandy blond who had the gun (he has no gun today) are all in there. Sandy blond looks at me with barely disguised anger. His knee is in a brace.

Sarah smiles. "There you are. We were just talking about you."

"I'm sure you were." (Freestanding chair still next to the window, which is not plate glass nor does it have mesh wiring in it to prevent shattering.)

"I was wondering if you might be willing to give us a better idea of what you did for the school and why they were so invested in you. You said you were 'hands'?"

"Hands, yes. Also stock predictor, corporate espionage specialist, fight picker, and resident scary psychotic chick."

Sarah looks sad. "I'm so sorry for everything you've been through. Would you like to talk about it?"

I stretch both shoulders, crack my neck, crack my knuckles. This is going to hurt. Nothing to be done for it. "Nope, don't want to talk about anything. You were using past tense to describe my work with Keane. You should use present tense. I *am* their hands."

"But—" Sarah looks confused. More evidence she shouldn't be doing this. She should look scared.

Cole understands. He quickly rises from the couch, puts himself between Sarah and me. Sandy blond is slower but he, too, stands, limps closer. I smile and hold both of my hands out wide.

"I really am sorry about this. But a girl's gotta do . . ." I lower my head and charge into Sandy blond, catching him around the middle and knocking him to the floor with a loud *oof.*

Cole picks me up and throws me off Sandy blond. I roll; my face smacks into the floor, hard. It will bruise. Good. I stand, shaking off the daze.

"I won't let you destroy this," Cole says. They need him. I'm so glad he's here.

"I'm not going to breathe a word about you." I swing at his head, making my movements obvious and wide. He ducks under my fist, slams his own into my face where I already hit it on the floor. I spin, hit the wall, use it to hold myself up.

Pain, pain, pain.

"I really am sorry." I look at Sarah, who is watching all this in horror. "And I promise not to tell them anything. But I've got to go."

I run for the window, twisting out of Cole's reach, then throw the chair through the glass with a resounding crash. Duck down, fist over my head again, kick out, Cole goes down, I see a knife on his belt.

I hit him in the nose, it's probably broken, then snake my hand out and slide the knife out of the sheath.

"Sofia, please." Sarah stands, holding her hands out. "You don't have to do this."

"No. I really do."

"Then walk out the door. We'll let you."

I laugh. She's so sweet. "Oh, I know. I just need physical evidence for a good escape story. I was knocked unconscious, kept in a cell, and fought my way out without speaking to a soul. I have no idea who took me. Good luck. Take care of Adam."

I climb out the window, letting the jagged edges of the glass catch on my arms, cut me. Then I run down the sidewalk.

Today is the end. Today I am done reacting. All these years I've been turning myself off, letting my paths choose themselves. After today I am *acting*. I am choosing.

I am going to do truly terrible things. Unthinkable things. But the back of my head is buzzing with right right right. I laugh, slide the knife into my pocket, and run toward the arch.

When I am close I pull out the stolen phone.

James answers immediately. "Fia? You escaped!" He must be with others if he's lying. "Where are you? We'll come get you."

"I want Annie underneath the arch. No one else. If anyone is with her, if anyone approaches her, I'll run and you'll never see me again."

"Come on, you know—"

"This is my only offer, James. Annie right underneath the

arch. I know you'll be watching. That's fine. But she needs to be by herself. You know I can't take her and run fast enough to get away. Tell them I'm confused and scared, and I need to see my sister, alone."

"Why?"

"Annie under the arch. Now." I put myself in the middle of a tour group, walk casually, circling closer. It's a beautiful day, clear blue sky. Warm. A day for endings and beginnings. I glance behind me. Cole is tracking me, trying to be invisible. That's fine. I look toward the arch and see a man—Darren from the hall—walk Annie to the center of the cement underneath. Then he looks all around and walks away. I watch him, trace him. No one can be too close. Annie looks so small. So alone.

Oh, Annie. Annie, Annie, Annie.

I will not cry. I will not be sorry. It has to be this way. It has to end. It's the only way to move forward.

I keep walking with the tour group. The arch park isn't crowded but it's steady with people, and that's enough. There is a man who has stopped to tie his shoelaces about twelve feet from Annie.

My phone is out again. "James. Tell the man tying his shoe to get away from my sister. Now."

He sighs. "Fine."

The man abruptly stands and walks away. I break from the group and sprint to close the distance. I know they've seen me now. I also know they'll hope that I'm going to come quietly after talking with my sister. Public disturbance is their last resort.

Annie looks so lost. I slow as I get close, walk up, drink in every detail of her. The brown hair kept simple at her shoulders. The china-doll mouth, exactly like mine. The squarer-face, delicate chin. The milky brown eyes looking out, looking out but seeing nothing.

She looks absolutely terrified.

I want to tell her it will be okay. But I can't lie, not about that. I reach out and take both her hands in mine, her soft, perfect, clean hands. She smiles, but tears are tracing out the corners of her eyes.

"Fia," she says. Her voice is strange, strained, choked. "I'm so sorry. For everything. But it's okay. I understand."

My stomach drops. She knows. She saw. Of course she saw. I wish I could tell her everything, but I can't. Not now, not ever. She saw and she still came. A sob rises in my throat, but I choke it back. This is right. I am choosing it.

"Annie," I whisper. "It's the only way. I can't protect you anymore, and we can never be free. Not together. I'm so sorry, but it's the only way." I let go of her hands, then lean forward and kiss her forehead. I want to stay here, frozen, with my sister, for all of time.

It's not an option.

I pull out the knife, and the sun catches it at an angle to glint like a beacon. I am going to lose my Annie forever. The sob comes out, but only just. "I love you. I love you, but I need you to be dead. You have to be dead."

I close the distance between us, the knife between our bodies, my hand behind her back supporting her in the last hug I will ever give her. And then I twist my wrist, and the knife cuts, cuts deep, my hand is wet with the blood. Annie gasps. "Be dead," I whisper so softly only her ears could ever hear it. "I'll miss you."

Then I step back and after a few seconds (please, please, Annie, understand, you have to understand what I'm doing) Annie puts her hands over her stomach and drops to the ground, unmoving. I hold the knife out to the side, the red red knife, and a drop falls to the ground from it.

And while anyone watching will be watching that hand, my other slips into my pocket, pulls out the tiny phone, and drops it onto Annie's hand, which quickly closes over it and then she doesn't move, not a hint of movement, good girl.

I smile, so proud of her, and say, "Good-bye, Annie. I love you."

Then I turn and walk away, toward where I know James will be waiting. After a dozen steps someone falls into place next to me, but I don't look at him. He doesn't matter. Someone else falls into step on my other side. I look back and see Cole running, dropping to Annie's side, putting a finger under her chin to look for a pulse.

We keep walking. I pass a trash can and drop the knife inside. No blood evidence for Keane. James takes the place of one of the men next to me, and whispers harshly, "Fia, what is wrong with you?"

I look at him and grin. "Absolutely nothing. The man by her body is from the group that kidnapped me. It was his knife. They'll clean up the mess. I'm free now to choose. And I choose Keane."

He's looking at me with horror—he has never looked at me this way—but then his eyes that pick up everything notice a deep gash across my stomach, the black T-shirt sliced open but hiding the blood. "What happened?" he asks, and I can see things falling into place behind his beautiful brown eyes. The angles. The showmanship of it all. The way Annie covered her stomach before falling.

"Had to jump out a window to get here. See?" I hold up my arms with their small cuts.

And then he smiles, and I know he knows what I did, and I know the secret will forever be safe with him because we will do this together. We will be inside Keane, farther inside than anyone else could ever get. And we will destroy his father and his webs of power and we will end this completely. I am giving up a life of freedom, I am giving up my sister, I am giving up who I could have been. But it's the right choice, because together James and I will do what no one else can. We will do what is right, however long and however much wrong it takes us to get there.

"I see." James laughs. "My clever girl."

Next to a van two men are holding Eden's arms, restraining her.

She shakes her head, tears spilling out of her eyes. "You're a monster. Annie never did anything to you, she loved you, and you . . . and you're happy and hopeful. James, you can't be okay with this." She looks at him for support, but he shrugs. She's shaking now, whether with tears or rage I couldn't say. "I can't—I'll be in the other car." She jerks her arms away from the men and walks quickly to the black sedan a few parking spots over, her gait stiff and unnatural.

I smile and James takes my hand that isn't covered in blood in his own. "Thank you," he whispers.

"It was the only way." I don't look back. I can't and I won't. I hope hope hope Annie and Adam will take care of each other. She'll figure out a way for all those women to be safe without Adam dying. I think that's what she was supposed to do all along.

And I think that this, here, with James, will always be wrong but it will always be the right sort of wrong, because if we don't do this, no one will. We are a matched set of perfect liars, perfectly destroyed people, perfect for destruction. James rubs his thumb down my own and my hand doesn't seem like it belongs on someone else anymore.

Annie is safe. And because *she* is, no one who hurt us will ever be safe again. I smile, and it is not a lie. It is a promise. I am ready.

ANNIE

Ten Years Ago

~

I'M NEARLY ASLEEP WHEN I FEEL THE BOTTOM OF MY bed move.

"Fia?"

I can hear her breathing; it's fast and ragged and peppered with sniffles. "Please?"

I sigh and scoot over to the wall, holding the covers open. Her little body snuggles in next to me. "Ouch!" I hiss as she knees me in the stomach.

"Sorry."

"You know you aren't allowed to do this."

"Please don't tell."

I smile. I won't. Because she'll get in trouble, but also because even though I pretend like I don't, I love it when Fia has nightmares and comes into my room. It makes me proud that she chooses me over our parents. "Okay," I say, patting her head and stroking her hair like Mom does to make me feel better.

"I wish night wasn't so long."

"Why?"

"It's scary. I can't see anything. What if there's something hiding in the dark in my room?"

"Silly. Dark isn't scary. Dark is safe."

"Why?"

"I live in the dark all the time. But when it's dark outside everyone has to be there, too. And if you can't see someone, they can't see you, either."

She sniffles a few times. "So, it's like *I'm* hiding in the dark?"

"Yes. You're the secret when it's dark. Dark is safe."

"Dark is safe," she whispers, snuggling into me and throwing one of her bony arms over my stomach. "But only with you here, too."

"Safe together." I smile and brush her hair away from where it's tickling my nose. Sometimes *I* am the one who takes care of Fia. It makes me happy. "I'll take care of you," I say, but she is already asleep. I breathe in the sweet shampoo scent of her and fall asleep, too.

Acknowledgments

~

FIRST THANKS, AS ALWAYS, TO MY NOAH, FOR HELPING me calm and organize the chaos that is my brain. You are everything good in my life. Thank you as well to my darling Elena and Jonah, for your patience when Mommy went crazy with a story. Again. You are absolutely delightful little people.

Thank you to my mom, Cindy, and my sister Lauren, for babysitting that one night so Noah and I could go on a date and see a movie that has absolutely nothing whatsoever to do with this but somehow sparked the idea that I needed. Please feel free to take credit for this book. Unless people hate it, in which case I guess you've just lost plausible deniability. Sorry.

Special thanks to my siblings, Erin, Lindsey, Lauren, and Matt. I am so glad to have grown up with you. All the memories and stolen clothes (Matt, you are exempted . . . I think) and shared history make me who I am, and I'm glad that you are all part of it. Again, feel free to take credit for me, unless people hate me; in which case, beat them up.

Biggest familial thanks go to my dad, for making me his Kick Butt Action Movie Buddy all growing up. KBP forever.

Thank you to Natalie Whipple, for always spurring me on and for saying, "I thought the sister would be the other POV?" I owe Annie to you. Among many other things (that are not imaginary people). Thank you to Shannon Messenger for doing a lightning-fast crit that I believe included threatening to throw olives (or was it carrots? I'd be much more frightened of carrots) at me. Thank you to Stephanie Perkins for always helping me find my way and for showing me where to deepen my stories and strengthen my writing. You're like my personal trainer, only instead of getting slender and toned I get better at writing. Maybe we should also try the slender and toned thing next time. Just a thought.

Thank you to Michelle Wolfson, Agent Extraordinaire, for letting me write a book I wasn't supposed to and for sending it out in spite of its being "crazy." You keep taking chances on me, and then you keep making those chances pay off. I am so glad you are in my life.

Thank you to Erica Sussman. I can't imagine making a book without you. I would make some funny threat about what I'd do if you ever quit being an editor, but after reading this book, you'd probably believe I was serious and get scared. I promise my love of working with and adoration of you is all things good and nonviolent. Thank you also to Berkeley, the cutest Harvard-bound dog in existence.

Thank you to the team at HarperTeen, including but not limited to Editorial Assistant of Awesome Tyler Infinger; Marketing Wonders Christina Colangelo and Stephanie Stein; Publicity Guru Casey McIntyre; Foreign Sales Phenoms Jean McGinley and Alpha Wong; Copyediting Ninja Jessica Berg; and Cover Design Demigods Alison Donalty and Michelle Taormina. I feel ridiculously fortunate that my professional life includes all of you.

Thank you to A. S. King, Nova Ren Suma, Marie Lu, and Franny Billingsley, who wrote books that made me think and in small ways informed this novel. Thank you to Snow Patrol, Muse, and the Civil Wars for writing songs that capture in a few minutes emotions I try to capture in a few (hundred) pages. Thank you to all the femmes fatales of literature, television, and film for being strong—and for the rare occasions those femmes fatales were also allowed to be human and deal with the consequences of impossible decisions.

Finally, thank you again, always, to my readers. You are all ridiculously good-looking and have impeccable taste in literature. Thanks for continuing to trust me by lending me your brains and imaginations for a few hours. You make my life awesome.